T0171690

CRASHES
AND
FRAUDS

JANNIE VELEZ

BALBOA.
PRESS

A DIVISION OF HAY HOUSE

Balboa Press books may be ordered through booksellers or by contacting:

Balboa Press
A Division of Hay House
1663 Liberty Drive
Bloomington, IN 47403
www.balboapress.com
1-(877) 407-4847

Because of the dynamic nature of the Internet, any Web addresses or links contained in this book may have changed since publication and may no longer be valid. The views expressed in this work are solely those of the author and do not necessarily reflect the views of the publisher, and the publisher hereby disclaims any responsibility for them.

The author of this book does not dispense medical advice or prescribe the use of any technique as a form of treatment for physical, emotional, or medical problems without the advice of a physician, either directly or indirectly. The intent of the author is only to offer information of a general nature to help you in your quest for emotional and spiritual well-being. In the event you use any of the information in this book for yourself, which is your constitutional right, the author and the publisher assume no responsibility for your actions.

ISBN: 978-1-4525-0107-9 (sc)
ISBN: 978-1-4525-0108-6 (e)

Any people depicted in stock imagery provided by Thinkstock are models, and such images are being used for illustrative purposes only.
Certain stock imagery © Thinkstock.

Printed in the United States of America

Balboa Press rev. date: 11/4/2010

CHAPTER 1:

He's Gone

"Chelsea, Shannon, Kelly, hurry up!" my mom said as we were racing out of the hospital parking lot to the hospital where my dad was barely staying alive. He was hooked up to a machine that was giving him oxygen, but I didn't know back then that it was called a ventilator, another machine that was giving him water, and third machine that was giving him a weird food-like substance that looked disgusting, but it looked like some of the doctors were getting ready to unhook all of the machines for good.

The whole reason why my dad was like this was because he got cancer. He started to develop the cancer while my mom was pregnant with Kelly. I don't remember what type of cancer it was called, but I remember that the type of cancer he got was giving him heart attacks everyday. We were lucky if we only got one heart attack One day a few years ago; his heart attack was so bad that it caused three organs to burst. My mom immediately called 911. Of course, this was a phone call my mom made everyday. Each time she called, she said the same thing. "This is May Bauber. We're coming."

Since the phone call was so common, we had to move out of our small apartment to a bigger house that was closer to the hospital, which made the drive faster. Even though it was a common ride, we were always in panic and fear.

My dad had his own room in the hospital and my mom had her own parking spot in the hospital parking lot. Since we went to the hospital everyday, we also had a specialized health insurance. We even had our own routine set up, but it was something that you wouldn't want for a routine. First, my mom got my sisters and me out of school if it was a week day. I f it was the weekend, we were home standing around him. Next, we jumped in the car and drove to the hospital, but on the weekends that was the first step. Then, we ran to my dad's room. Finally, my dad got in his bed with the help of doctors as we stood near him. We all told him that we were there for him as we held his hands.

Sadly, we were at our last visit. "This may be his last day, Mrs. Bauber," the doctor said. "His heart rate is going slower than ever and we don't know how long we can keep him alive."

"No!" my little sister Kelly screamed. A kid like her was able to understand that her dad was dying. She tried to hold back her tears, but she couldn't, so she ran out of the room and ran straight to the car.

"C'mon dad," I said. "Don't go yet." All I wanted was to hear my dad to say something back to me, but I knew that he couldn't. He turned his head to look at me. I knew that he wanted to tell me something, but when he opened his mouth, no words came out, so I gave him his notepad and a pen. He took the pen and started to write something on the notepad. He gave me the notepad, but his motor skills were so bad that his writing was illegible. I felt like crying, but I couldn't.

Suddenly, my dad's heart rate stopped. At 4:20 p.m., on December 20, 2007, my dad, Samuel Bauber, was officially dead. I really felt like crying at that moment, but I still couldn't cry.

"No!" my sister Chelsea screamed. She said that exactly how Kelly said it, even though Chelsea was my older sister.

"Chelsea," my mom said, "I want you to take your sisters home. I think I'm going to stay here for a while. I'll come home when I'm ready."

I was glad my mom said that. I couldn't stand to see a dead body, especially if it was my dad, but for some strange reason, I couldn't stop looking at him.

"Shannon, let's go," Chelsea said. I didn't even say anything. I just followed her out of the room as she pulled me out, but I wasn't even walking anymore. Even as I was dragged out of the room, the picture of my dad lying dead was still in my head as if I was still in the room.

Even though Chelsea had her driving license, her driving was horrible. I had always thought that she used a bribe to get her license. I couldn't believe that she had never gotten a ticket before, but that last the last thing on my mind.

"Do you think that Dad will go to heaven?" Kelly asked after about a minute. "Do you think it was painful when Dad died?"

After she asked ten different unanswerable questions, I was so aggravated that I came out of my trauma and I had to say, "Kelly, I don't know! Shut up, I don't feel like answering these questions right now." I think I yelled at her too much though, because I thought I heard her about to cry, but I thought it was better than her questions because there was finally silence. It was good thing that we were almost home because I wanted to run to my room and cry into my pillow on my bed. I wanted to cry in the car, but I was supposed to be a good role model big sister for her, which I had just ruined by yelling at her.

I handed off the big sister role model to Chelsea, and she answered all of Kelly's questions. I didn't want to hear their conversation, so I pulled my earphones out of my pocket and turned up the volume all the way. I didn't have the urge to cry anymore. My mind was too occupied with my favorite song, but I had a felling that I was going to damage my eardrums from the noise.

CHAPTER 2:

Start Packing

After about twenty-four hours since we left the hospital, my mom called. I wanted to answer it and talk to her. She was the only one in the house that I could pour out all my emotions to. In stead, Chelsea answered the phone.

She said, "Hello, Chelsea. I think I'm going to stay here at the hospital for a few more days. The doctors here are going to pay for all the funeral costs for your father. Do you or Shannon or Kelly want to come?" The sorrow was still easily heard in here voice. The only way I knew that was because I was standing right next to Chelsea.

"Let me talk to her," I whispered.

Then she said to me, "Shut up. Oh, not you Mom, but they don't want to go." I thought that she would have at least asked us, but, honestly, I didn't want to go to a funeral. "I actually had another plan. I've been looking at some brochures, and since it's winter break, I thought it'll be nice to take Shannon and Kelly to this really cool ski lodge in Nevada that I can pay for with my own money. It might help them to stop thinking about you-know-who if they're skiing down some slopes. What do you think?"

"That sounds fine," my mom replied. "That's actually would work better than having them go to a funeral. I want you girls to continue being happy and don't let it ruin your regular lives. All I ask of you is to make sure you come back before school starts again and you don't take my credit card. I don't want to come home hearing of unreported absences and credit debt."

"Okay, Mom," Chelsea said. "If I set up reservations now, I think we could leave as soon as tomorrow. We'll see you when we get back."

Then she hung up and came to my room that I shared with Kelly. "Hey, do you two want to go to a ski lodge?" She asked.

"Sure," I said. "When do we leave?"

"We leave tomorrow morning at nine," Chelsea said. "You should pack your bags now so you can go to sleep early."

"That plan sounded good to me," I said

"I don't want to wake up early," Kelly whined. "The point is to sleep in during winter break." Then Chelsea left our room.

"Do you need help packing your suitcase, Kelly?" I said an hour later as I peeked in her room.

"I'm nine years old, Shannon. I can pack my own suitcase," Kelly said as she closed the door.

I went to Chelsea's room and opened the door without knocking and asked her, "Can you bring down the suitcases?"

"You're so useless," she said. "You can get it down yourself. And don't come in my room without permission.

Chelsea helped us get some suitcases down from the attic. She grabbed the biggest one for herself and had me share the smallest one with Kelly. I should have taken down the suitcases myself, then I could have gotten the biggest suitcase for me and had Chelsea share the smallest one with Kelly. Even though Kelly said she didn't want my help, I still picked out her clothes. None of the clothes she picked were suitable for snowy weather, whereas I, on the other hand, picked out the most suitable clothes because I was smarter.

5

While I was stuck at home packing for the ski lodge, Chelsea went across the street to Terra's house.

"Where are you going?" I asked.

"Terra's throwing me a party," She said as she opened the door. "All of the teenagers are invited except you."

"Don't you need to pack?"

"No, that's your job. Now get to it or I tell Mom you broke her vase."

She left the house Terra's. Terra Carter was Chelsea's best friend forever ever since they met in preschool, even though Chelsea was girly and Terra was a tomboy. Chelsea wanted to bring Terra along on the trip, but Terra wasn't allowed to go. They both promised to call each other everyday that they were in separate states. Both forgot that it would be long distances call, and I knew that Chelsea would have made me pay for the calls, and the calls would have been long.

Since Chelsea still had the night to be with Terra, they made the best of it, which was why Terra set up a party at the last minute. I didn't know what they were doing, but I heard the music from my room, and when I looked outside, the pizza delivery guy was carrying ten pizzas.

I would have gone next door to visit to Woody Parker. He was my boyfriend. He was my friend ever since I met him when I was four years old. When we were twelve years old, and I had just gotten out of a really bad relationship, we decided to start dating. We thought it wouldn't work out at first because he was really smart and I was a slacker, but we gave it a try anyway. At that time, we had been dating for almost a whole year and everyone in the eighth grade knew about us. Since I had to watch Kelly and I couldn't leave the house, I just called him instead.

"Hi, Woody," I said. "I know it's sort of last minute, but I'm going out of town for a few days."

"I know," he said. "I noticed the party at Terra's house. She was going to invite me, but Chelsea wouldn't let her. Anyway, I'm glad you called me to make sure I knew and I'll miss you."

"I'll miss you too, but how about if we call each other everyday? Tomorrow I'll call you and then the day after that you'll call me, and we'll keep that going until I come back."

"But you said you're only going to be gone for a few days."

"Yeah, but I don't know how long I'll be gone. Chelsea made the reservations, but didn't tell me what they were."

"Okay."

"Wait, there's one more thing. Can you pay for the calls? I'm broke." I had money, but I knew it would all go to Chelsea's long distant calls.

"Sure." Then we hung up.

Even though I didn't know how long I would be gone, I also didn't know that we would see each other sooner than we thought.

CHAPTER 3:

We're leaving

"Kelly, are you ready yet?" I yelled as I knocked on the door annoyingly. "You've been in the bathroom forever and Chelsea said we're leaving at nine! C'mon!"

"Okay, okay," Kelly said as she came out of the bathroom, "I'm out. Are you happy now? You should know that beauty takes time."

"Kelly, you don't know what beauty is, so it doesn't matter how you look," Chelsea said as she came downstairs, and I agreed with Chelsea. We only got along when we were teasing Kelly. Then she looked at her suitcase. "Hey, you packed everything I needed. I guess I won't break Mom's vase after all, and you can finish getting ready in the car if you need to." I don't know why she said that when Kelly and I were ready.

I helped put the suitcases in the car because no one else helped, and also because Chelsea threatened me again by saying, "If you don't put the suitcases in the trunk, I'll hide a spider in one of your meals, and you won't know which meal." It was strange that she threatened me a second time in the same week. Usually, she only threatened me once a week.

Right before I got in the car, Woody came out. He gave me a quick hug and gave me a goodbye kiss. Terra also came by to give Chelsea a goodbye hug and an air kiss right before she opened the car door. Kelly just sat in the car because she said that her friends lived far away, but we all knew that she was too weird to have any friends. After we all said our goodbyes, Chelsea told Kelly and me to get in the car and buckle up. We all gave one last wave goodbye and Chelsea backed out of the driveway, and this time she backed out without hitting any cars.

"Remember, I'll call you!" I yelled to Woody as I rolled down the window.

"Roll up the window," Chelsea said. "You're letting the heat get out."

"Hey Shannon," Kelly whispered a few minutes later.

I backed up my seat and turned around. "What?"

"Why do you let Chelsea walk over you?"

"It's for the same reason I walk all over you. If I didn't pack her suitcase, she would have broken Mom's favorite vase and blame me. And the joke's on her. I only packed small weights in there and filled the rest with toilet paper to fill the empty space."

"That is good. But wait, what about when she opens her suitcase and sees what you've done?"

"I got it all planned out. When she's all mad about it, I'll just call Mom and tell her that Chelsea was using her credit card."

Then she silently laughed and thought for a few seconds and asked, "Hey, when have you ever walked all over me?"

"Um... never, but I want you to remember this. I'm a nice big sister, but a mean little sister, so I'll never take advantage of you."

"Okay, can I turn on the TV now?" Kelly asked.

"Sure," Chelsea said. We had a TV that had all cable channels and a DVD player. It was a gift. We weren't able to afford expensive things since our dad didn't work and the welfare check was small. Kelly dug around on the floor looking for her favorite DVD.

"Are you sure we didn't leave anything at home or leave any lights on?" Chelsea asked. "We can still go back. I haven't gotten on the freeway yet. It's not too late."

"No," I replied. I remembered checking the entire house and I turned off everything. I even made sure that I packed everything we would need for that trip, except for Chelsea's belongings. More importantly, I put a first aid kit and a rope under Chelsea's seat, and I made sure to tell Chelsea about it.

"Are we there yet?" Kelly asked after three hours.

"Kelly," Chelsea said trying not to yell at her, "we're driving from Los Angeles to Carson City, which is all the way in Nevada. This trip is going to take about ten hours, maybe more with traffic. We won't be at the ski lodge until like seven at night. I don't want to hear you saying, 'Are we there yet?' until then. Shannon, make sure Kelly doesn't watch the PG-13 movies."

"How am I supposed to do that?" I asked. "I'm sitting in the front seat. I can't see the TV in the backseat."

"That's why you use your ears to listen," she said. "Isn't that obvious?"

"Actually, I think I won't want TV," Kelly said.

"Fine, then shut up!" Chelsea and I yelled at the same time.

Kelly was quiet for the rest of the trip. Actually, all three of us were so quiet that we could hear the car's engine, which meant that we were all very quiet.

The silence ended two hours later when Chelsea's cell phone rang. It was Terra. I didn't know why Terra called. She should have known that Chelsea would still be driving.

"Don't answer your phone, you're driving," I said. "Use the Bluetooth instead."

"I know that," she said, "but I can drive and talk and I don't know where the Bluetooth is. Nothing's going to happen, so shut up."

"Okay, but if you get a ticket, Mom will take away your car keys."

"Like I care. I'll find them someway, and I thought I told you to shut up." Then she answered her phone. I just lied back in my seat and listened to the songs that Woody got me for my birthday. When I turned around to see why Kelly was so quiet, I noticed that she had fallen asleep. I thought it would be better if I put on my earplugs and listen to something that I liked than to listen to Chelsea's conversation, and I knew from past experiences that Chelsea and Terra can talk for hours without any topic. They had that talent since they were twelve years old.

CHAPTER 4:

The Cell Phone

"Hey Terra!" Chelsea said. "I can't believe I forgot to tell you happy birthday. I don't know how I could've forgotten about that. I'm so sorry. Maybe I can make it up by throwing you a birthday party." When I looked at her face, she even looked sorry, but at the same time, I looked nervous. She had one hand holding the cell phone to her ear and the other hand on the wheel, and her hand on the wheel didn't look like it could hold it.

"It's okay," Terra replied. "I know that you forgot. The party that I had yesterday was my birthday party. I had a feeling that you'd be thinking about your dad, so it's okay that you forgot."

"Thanks, you're a good friend."

"But more importantly, I just got some bad news and some good news. Both of them are related to each other. Which one do you want to hear first?"

"I don't know. I guess I'll hear the bad news. Wait; is the bad news about you or me? Do I need to worry about me?"

"The bad news about me and the good news is about Shannon and me, so you don't have to worry. I know your don't want worry lines. So, which one do you want to hear first, the good news or the bad news?"

"Well, since it's not about me, I still want to hear the bad news first. I want to get it out of the way." The conversation started to sound interesting and I noticed that there was a topic. Those conversations were rare, so I decided to lower the volume on my earphones, and I slightly pulled them out just enough to listen without Chelsea noticing.

"So do I. As you know, I'm seventeen now. It was supposed to be a happy day for me, but I got a call from the owner of the skate park. He told me that I only have one year to…to…be queen of the skate park! I can't believe my six-year reign is coming to an end!" Terra is a major skateboarder like me and she had been queen since she was twelve. For nine years, it was my dream to be queen of the skate park, but I knew that the only way that would have happened is if Terra chose me to be princess of the skate park.

"What are you going to do?"

"Well, here's the good news. I know that all past skate park queens and kings became famous. So, in one year from now, some sports scouts are going to see me only once and if they think I'm good, I will be famous. Also, I have one year to find and train a skate park princess or prince. This kid has to be a big fan of skateboarding, a member of the skateboard club for at least two years, and currently in middle school. Suddenly, I remembered that your sister Shannon is all these things. Once you come back, Shannon has to go to the skate park every weekend for three hours of training until I turn eighteen. Of course, she will have to skateboard to the skate park. She'd be considered a disgrace if you or your mom drive her to he skate park. Okay?"

"That's a lot of information, but okay." She hung up immediately and pulled my ear phones out of my ears. She told me everything. Even though I heard the news twice, I still acted as if I only heard it once. For some reason, it sounded better when it was told directly to me. I didn't usually scream, but that was a special occasion. This scream had to be the loudest scream ever. I actually screamed so loud that for a second, Chelsea let go of the wheel.

"You really need to control your screams," Chelsea said.

"Yeah," Kelly said. "You scared away all the birds and you almost cracked the windows."

"Well, I'm sorry about the birds and the windows," I said sarcastically. I really didn't care about the birds and I knew I wouldn't have cracked the windows with a scream. The windows were way too thick.

"Why don't you just text Terra telling her how excited you are," Chelsea said as she looked around. "Does anyone know where my cell phone is?"

"Yeah," I said. "I think you dropped it when I screamed, but you can look for it later."

"No, you look for my cell phone while I drive. You were the one who screamed, not me."

"Well, I don't know where you dropped it, so it would be easier if you looked for it. You just need to remember how it fell out of your hand."

"Okay, then at least hold the wheel while I look for it, but I didn't pay attention to how I dropped it. I was too busy driving."

"Forget the phone. It's not that important. I'll just wait until we get to a pit stop, and then you can look for it."

"No, I need to find the phone now. It's very important. What if someone wants to call me while I'm driving? You don't think that's important? Just hold the wheel."

"I can't do that. I don't have a driver's license and I don't know how to drive. Why can't you pull over?"

"I can't pull over. I'm in the middle lane and there are too many cars in the next lane, so hold on to the wheel."

I gave up the argument because I was getting tired of the bickering, even though it was usual for us to bicker, except we didn't bicker that long, so I decided to hold on to the wheel. First I thought to turn the wheel really fast to freak out Chelsea, but then I realized that would me immature. Also, I probably wouldn't have timed it right and I would've hit a car, and then it would have been my fault if anyone got injured.

CHAPTER 5:

Crash!

While Chelsea was looking for her cell phone and I was holding on to the wheel, I noticed that she missed her turn. I would have turned the wheel myself, but I didn't know how much I was supposed to turn it, and I knew that I was supposed to put on the turn signal, but I didn't know how to do that either. I also thought that I would have had to speed up if I wanted to make a U-turn, but my feet couldn't reach the pedal and I didn't know how much I should have pushed the pedal. So, I just sat in the passenger seat holding on to the wheel that Chelsea should have been holding.

If we didn't make a U-turn soon, I knew that we wouldn't have made it to Carson City in time and we would have had to get new directions. I just wished that I could get Chelsea's attention and to get her to turn around and to stop thinking about finding her phone, and my wish came true. I was able to inform her about it, but I then I really wished that I had rephrased what I said, and I still regret about not rephrasing.

"Chelsea," I said, "you missed your turn. We need to turn around."

"What?" she said as she sat up.

"I said that you missed you turn, so turn the car around" I repeated louder.

Chelsea quickly looked up, pushed my hands off of the wheel, put her hands on the wheel, and jerked the wheel to turn right instead of left. Suddenly, I noticed that she didn't mean to turn the wheel. She just moved so fast that her hand hit the wheel accidentally which made the wheel turn by itself. She wasn't even looking at the road and she was probably still thinking about where she dropped her phone. If she had turned left, she could have made a U-turn and continue driving toward the exit that she missed. She turned right. She noticed what she did, so she tried to turn left, but she wasn't fast enough. The car turned, which left the car hanging by the front wheels. She went off the road, and since the road was on a bridge, fell off the bridge! The front wheels of the car were barely hanging on to the railing, which caught the attention of many drivers.

This bridge wasn't as high as ordinary bridges. This bridge was much higher. It was so high that you could see so much detail on a plane that flies by. The only way that I knew that was because when I looked up, I saw a plane.

Right at this moment, we were screaming harder than ever.

"What do we do?!" Kelly cried, and I really mean that she cried.

"I know!" Chelsea said quickly. She immediately pulled out the emergency rope from under the seat. She threw the rope over the railing and got out of the car to tie the rope on the railing of the bridge, but she was only able to tie it if she completely came out of the car. This was going perfect except for one small problem. She forgot to get Kelly and me and the car fell even more off the railing. There was a giant crowd of people staring at us. Only one wheel was on the railing. Luckily, she remembered about us.

"Reach my hand!" she said to me. "Leave everything in the car! I don't about the luggage and my phone, just get Kelly, and grab my hand!" While she was talking, I could tell that she really meant it. I could tell that she didn't care about her phone. So, I grabbed Kelly's hand and climbed to the driver's seat. I was just another few inches away from Chelsea's hand, but my other was on the seat and it slipped. I fell to the backseat on top of Kelly and the impact was too much. The next thing I knew was that the car was falling and I was on death road.

I couldn't do anything except to get off of Kelly before I became the reason for killing her. It's true that your life flashes before your eyes, because that's what happened to me, but it was short since I was only thirteen. Since Kelly and I were in the falling car together and I had a feeling that the car would be falling for at least a minute, I said, "Kelly, before we die, I want to tell you that-" That was all I was able to say. We ended up hitting the ground sooner than I thought. I didn't get a chance to tell her what I wanted to tell her.

This wasn't like in a movie where you see heaven when you are in a crash or some other type of near death experience. I didn't see anything like heaven, but I thought that I really was dead, and I was so sure that I would be dead. It was so logical that I would have died, but apparently my logic isn't good because I thought I would fall for about a minute. Of course, I wasn't actually thinking about anything at the time. Actually, I was completely unconscious, so I didn't know how long I was lying there, but if I was on a road, I was probably moved soon after the crash, and my guess is that Kelly was also unconscious.

Above the bridge, Chelsea was fine without a single scratch. She knew that her cell phone was long gone, so she said, "Someone call 911! My little sisters are in that car!" Actually, I don't know if that even happened. I'm just guessing, but I do hope that's how it happened or if something else like that happened. She probably used a call box nearby for emergency, since that was an emergency. If she hadn't, she would have been a horrible person and I would have died. All I know for sure is that Chelsea was unharmed, or at least she was hurt, but not hurt enough that she would have needed to be hospitalized for a long period of time.

CHAPTER 6:

Back in the Hospital

It wasn't until the next day when I finally woke up. I know this place, I thought as I slowly opened my eyes. I recognized that the photos on the nearby table were the same photos from my dad's room. The photos on the table were of my mom, my dad, Chelsea, and me. It always made him feel better to see himself before he was hospitalized, which was why I was only four years old, Chelsea was only eight years old, and Kelly wasn't born yet. Suddenly, I realized that I was in the hospital in what used to be my dad's room. I didn't know what was going on, or why I was in my dad's bed.

"Oh, she's awake!" I was able to recognize my mom's voice. She walked over to me and hugged me, which is something that she rarely did.

"Mom," I said. "Where's Kelly?" When I said that, I didn't remember who Kelly was or why I said that, but I was having the hardest time to remember anything.

"She's in another room. She just woke up from her coma a few hours ago, and we were waiting for you to wake up. You were in a coma for an entire day. I came as soon as Chelsea called me." I was so glad to hear that Kelly was alive, and that I was alive. I was also glad that my mom finally put us first instead of work, but I couldn't believe that she only came when we heard that we were in the hospital. If Chelsea wouldn't have called her, she would have never called us.

"So how is she?" I asked, trying not to think about my mom neglecting us.

"She's paralyzed from the waist down." Even though I was happy for Kelly being alive, at the same time I felt very sorry for her. I didn't know that a car crash could result in paralysis, but at least it's better than dying. "The doctors said that you have to stay still for a very long time."

"What do you mean? Can I at least stand up?" Even though I asked, I didn't need an answer. I noticed that I was hooked up to a ventilator that was next to me and there was a long tube connected to me. It was probably on my neck and I just couldn't see it or feel it. When I tried to get up, I couldn't. Then I realized that I couldn't get up because I was paralyzed! I couldn't believe that I, of all the people in the world, was paralyzed. I was supposed to be the skate park princess. The only thing I was able to move was my head and my neck. My entire body was actually stiff as a board. I almost felt complete hatred toward Chelsea. It was her fault that I was in the hospital.

Not long after talking to my mom, the doctors put me in a wheelchair that I had to stand on. The wheel chair was supposed to prevent be from getting bed sores. I was only standing because I was strapped to it. At least it was better than being bedridden.

"I'm here, Shannon!" Woody came in the room, but it took me a minute to remember who he was. He must have heard about the crash. "It's worse than I thought! How long will you be like this?"

"Forever!" I replied. "I can only move my head, but I can still kiss." Right when I was about to kiss Woody, the doctors put glass walls around me.

"Time for your shower," one of the doctors said. Apparently, I had to take showers in my wheelchair. I also had to sleep and do everything in my wheelchair.

"Will I be able to go back to school again?" I asked.

"No," my mom said. "You will stay here at the hospital and a tutor will come by for six hours."

"Six hours is as long as regular school."

"I know. You will do the same amount of work as you would do just like regular school, which means you still have to wake up at the same time that you would for regular school."

"That's not fair. Shouldn't there be like an exception? I'm paralyzed!"

"Most of your body is paralyzed, but not your brain."

"Okay, but what about Kelly?"

"She needs to be tested so the doctors know more about her paralysis. So until her testing is over, she will get the same treatment as you. It's time to take your shower now."

This shower was the strangest shower I had ever taken. On top of me, there was a hose put in the walls. Water didn't come out of it though. It was more like a deep mist being sprayed at me. I'm glad that the shower was only ten minutes long because I was already getting bored by the fifth minute. I would have looked bored, but that was impossible. After my shower, the hose was replaced with a different hose that blew hot air at me so I could dry off.

After I was dried and the walls were removed, I asked Woody, "Will you visit me everyday?"

"Of course," he said. "I'll come by everyday in the afternoon, and when school starts again, I'll come by after school and on Saturdays I'll take you to the skate park, if that's all right with you."

"That sounds nice, but the skate park is closed right now and it won't reopen until the Saturday after school starts."

"Okay, then when I visit on Saturday, we'll just hang out here. How does that sound."

"That's good. Thanks Woody," I was glad to hear that he was still going to think about me. I was worried that he would forget about me like I was nothing anymore, but he didn't. I knew that there was no way that I was going into depression as long as Woody was around.

CHAPTER 7:

Merry Christmas

After Woody left, I didn't know what to do. I turned my head to look at the calendar on the wall, and I noticed that it was December 23rd. Then it occurred to me that it was the day before Christmas Eve. Why didn't anyone tell me? I thought.

Just like most kids, Christmas was the one day of the year that I looked forward to every year. Then, I started to think about the presents I would get and how happy all five of us would be. Suddenly, I started to cry silently and I remembered that my dad just died a few days before and everyone was probably still mourning about him, and now everyone was also worried about Kelly and me because of our paralysis. The happiness was gone, and I felt bad to think about presents and happiness, but I just wanted everything to go back to normal. I tried to stop crying before anyone noticed because I didn't want anyone to see me.

I tried to stop thinking about Christmas and happiness, but that was very hard to do, especially because there was a happy holiday movie on TV. I turned my head so I wouldn't see the TV, but that only left me to stare at the ceiling. I wanted to look outside, but the curtains were closed. For the next few hours, I continued to stare at the ceiling, and I had no choice but to let my tears dry on my face. I thought about nothing at all until night came and I fell asleep again.

It was December 24th, the busiest shopping day of the year. When I woke up, Chelsea was standing in front of me with five different shopping bags from different stores. "Guess who went shopping?" Chelsea asked.

I didn't want to talk to her. I still felt like I hated her and I felt like I would never talk to her. I know I wasn't supposed to hate family, but I couldn't forgive her. I was thinking that the crash wasn't my fault, but it was her fault.

Chelsea came closer and said, "Say something. I get it, you're mad at me, but you can't shun me. At least ask me what I bought."

"What did you buy?" I asked. Somehow, I was able to talk to her.

"Can't tell you, but you'll find out when I give you your present tomorrow."

"How can you shop at a time like this? Dad just died!"

Chelsea put down her bags and said, "Hey, don't be upset. I know Dad just died, but we can't let that ruin Christmas. I already talked to Mom and she said that it's okay if I went shopping with Terra, so I've been at the mall for hours. I worked out this plan with Terra so everyone gets two gifts. Hey, cheer up, okay?"

"Okay," I said.

As she left the room, she said, "If you want to hate me, go ahead. I know I can't blame you if you do." Then she grabbed her bags and walked out the room.

Wait," I said, and that got her attention. "You're wrong."

"What?"

"You can blame me for what happened. On the night before we left home, I didn't want to pack your suitcase. So, I filled it with weights to make it feel heavy. If I didn't put in clothes instead of weights, the car probably wouldn't have fallen when I slipped."

She stared at me in silence, and then she ran out of the room. She went to Kelly's room and I heard her say the same thing. Then

I didn't feel like hating her anymore, but instead that she should had hated me.

Later in the afternoon, Woody came by to see me, which was such a relief.

"How are you doing today?" he asked.

"Okay," I didn't want to tell him that I cried because I didn't want him to feel sympathetic for me. I also didn't tell him what I told Chelsea, so instead I asked, "Why didn't you tell me what day it was yesterday?"

"I didn't want you to find out because I wanted to surprise you tomorrow. How'd you find out?"

"Chelsea and her shopping bags told me."

He had a quick laugh and said, "I heard that since you can't come home, we are going to celebrate here in your room. All we have to do is decorate the place and bring Kelly here. Or would you prefer if Kelly wasn't here? I'm bringing the mistletoe."

I had a quick laugh too, and then I said, "I can't wait."

Woody looked at the clock and said, "I have to go now, but I'll see you tomorrow morning." He gave me a kiss on the cheek and said, "Even in that hospital gown, you still look hot." Then he left with a very good thought in my mind.

At night, I had a dream that it was already Christmas, but it was completely miserable and nothing that I had expected. Everyone was dressed in black and they were all sad. Chelsea's shopping bags filled with presents were burning in a fireplace that came out from nowhere. Worse of all, Woody was tearing up the mistletoe. The nightmare was so bad that I had to wake myself up. I forced my eyes to open, but when they were open, I realized that it was only the middle of the night. I closed my eyes again hoping to have a better dream until morning.

Luckily, by the time I woke up for the second time, it was already Christmas morning, and everyone was there. Mom, Chelsea, Woody, Terra, and Kelly were all there. The entire room was decorated in red and green and there were piles of presents under the Christmas tree. Best of all, Woody was standing there smiling with the mistletoe. It was better than I had imagined. It was just like any other traditional Christmas. I never wanted that wonderful day to end.

CHAPTER 8:

Back to School

Unfortunately, Christmas had to come to an end along with the rest of winter break, which also ended the holiday cheer, so I went back to being sad about paralysis. I knew that the holidays and winter break weren't going to last forever. Nothing happened during the following week of winter break, but for some reason, it seemed to go by too quickly, which was probably why school started sooner than when I wanted it to be. I woke up around seven in the morning, even though I really didn't want to. A nurse helped me to get dressed while another nurse helped me brush my hair.

Since my new classroom was in a different room across the hall, I had to wear a smaller version of a ventilator. It was still a ventilator, except it went under my shirt and the tube to my neck was smaller, so it wasn't visible through my shirt. I was supposed to wear it whenever I had to leave my room, and nobody even noticed that I was wearing it. It was made so people like me with limited mobility were a little less limited with mobility, so we could breathe outside of our hospital rooms. I was breathing differently though, because on the smaller tube.

"Shouldn't Kelly be here for school too?" I asked. I knew that Kelly was one of those kids who didn't want to go to school, but when she gets there, she was glad that she went. She was always like that when I was in elementary school with her, but she could've changed since I graduated three years earlier.

"She is," one of the nurses said. "She's in another room for school since she's in fourth grade and you're in eighth grade. It's just for academic reasons."

We didn't start school until eight since it was supposed to be regular school, so I still had another half an hour with nothing to do. I just stood in my wheel chair watching the news.

"Can I talk to Kelly?" I asked one of my nurses about twenty minutes later. I didn't care to talk to Kelly, but I was so bored that I couldn't take it.

"Of course," she said, and she took me to Kelly's classroom.

"Do you think I would ever be able to go back to regular school again?" Kelly asked as soon as I was in her room.

"Of course," I replied, but I wasn't sure, so I made it up as I was talking. "Well, I know you'll get back to school when your testing is done. You can actually use you hands! But for me, I think I'll be stuck here until I graduate from college."

"When will I be able to see my friends?" Kelly asked.

"You'll see them when you go back to regular school," I said. "Until then, you could always call your friends." I laughed. "You have no friends, so stop lying, weirdo." Kelly wasn't insulted by my remark since I had been teasing her for years. Our conversation had to end because it was five minutes until eight.

This school was exactly like real school. There was still the huge similarity: I found the classes very boring. The only difference I could find was that I was the only student since there weren't any other paralyzed eight graders, someone else was writing for me since I couldn't use my hands, and that I could blurt out the answers to every question since I couldn't raise my hand, but most of the time, I didn't even know what the answers were because I didn't listen.

Okay, so there were three differences, but it still seemed like regular school. Oh yeah, and a fourth difference would be that I had no desk. I just stood in my wheelchair in the middle of the room. It was still school though. I just had to go through this for the rest of the week, and possibly just like I told Kelly, until I graduate from college.

The first day back to school was just as slow as real school and it included all the same classes. After school, Woody came by just like he promised. That was the fifth difference. I didn't get to pass notes to Woody during every class, even though when I used to pass notes, we would get in trouble when we got caught.

But there was one thing that I missed the most about going to school. I missed the popularity. I was popular for two reasons: I was the first seventh grader to started dating, and the school was founded by my grandfather, which was why the school was called Bauber Junior High.

"How was school?" I asked him. Surprisingly, all the things he did at school, I did at school.

"Okay, that's freaky," he said. "I think the nurses are contacting your teachers and we both did the same things because we have the exact same classes."

"That does kind of explain a lot. Well, I just have to get through four more days and then you can take me to the skate park. This week is the reopening and I can't wait. I heard from Terra that the skate park was extended. Everything was repainted and there are some new ramps to fill the new extension. She also told me that there is another special surprise."

"I can't wait either. So, what time should I pick you up?"

"I don't know, probably sometime in the afternoon, so I can see it when everyone is there."

So, for the next four days while I sat in school, instead of paying attention to the lessons, I just looked like I was listening when I was actually thinking about going to the skate park and finding out what the special surprise was. My guess was that the special surprise was a visit from a professional skater, or something else that would change my life. I knew in my heart that the skate park was where I rightfully belonged. That's what Terra always used to say to me when I was little, and I always believed that even though I didn't understand what it meant to belong to a skate park when I was little.

CHAPTER 9:

The Skate Park

"Okay, the skate park members know nothing about my injury. I can't believe I forgot about that. So, I came up with a plan," I said to Woody at the hospital. "When we enter the skate park, you'll glue my shoes to my skateboard, take me out of my wheelchair, and hold my hand as Chelsea pushes me to look like I skateboarded from home to here. I'll be wearing my mobile ventilator, so no one will see it. That's why I'm wearing a turtle neck today."

"That's doable," Woody said. "Now we just need permission to take you out of the hospital."

"That's easy," I said. "Just ask one of my nurses and tell them you are going to take me out on a date. They already know that you're my boyfriend. Just say that and be honest."

"Okay," Woody said. He walked over to my nurse and said, "I'm Woody, Shannon's boyfriend, and I just wanted to know if I can take Shannon out on a date."

"Sure Woody," the nurse said, "as long as she doesn't eat anything and she needs to be back by seven. If anything goes wrong, you're responsible for it."

"Okay," Woody said.

We didn't leave the hospital until two, when everyone was at the skate park. The plan worked perfectly. Chelsea drove Woody and me to the skate park, but she had to park on the street because the skate park had no parking lot. Once we got out of the car, Chelsea got me out my wheelchair, Woody put glue on my shoes, and he quickly put my skateboard on my shoes before the glue dried. He held my hand and Chelsea gave me a hard push. It didn't matter how hard the push was because I didn't feel it. But Woody quickly pulled me back.

"This isn't going to work," he said. "At the speed you go at, I won't be able to catch up with you, I'll let go, and you'll fall over. I think I know how to solve this problem. Chelsea, check the car for another skateboard."

Chelsea checked the car and she found another skateboard. "I found one," she said.

"Now get the glue," he said. He put glue on his shoes and pressed the skateboard on his shoes. "I'm going to skateboard with you, which means that Chelsea will need to push the both of us."

"But those are your good shoes," I said.

"I'll do anything for you," Woody said.

"You're so sweet!" I said. Since he was so sweet, I gave him a kiss.

"Are you ready yet?" Chelsea said. "Your fans are waiting."

"We're ready," I said with a giant confident smile.

"Okay," Chelsea said, "One, two, three!"

Her push was strong enough to push us, making it look like we skateboarded all the way to the skate park. Our plan went perfectly. When my fans saw me, Terra cued them to applaud and she gave an announcement. She said, "Skateboarders, meet your new princess, Shannon Bauber! Today, she brought her boyfriend, Woody Parker! He's also a fellow skateboarder." The part about Woody being a skateboarder was a lie. Woody didn't know a thing about skateboarding.

I looked around at the skate park, and Terra was right. Everything was repainted in a really nice shade of blue. On every ramp, there was the logo of the skate park's sponsor. As we skated up the ramp, I noticed how much bigger the skate park looked.

"Now, is there anyone with questions for Shannon or Woody?" When Terra said that, so many people had their hands up. "Okay, you sir."

"Shannon, can you tell us why you are going to be queen, and no one else is?" The person who said that was another teen who wanted to be king.

Terra knew that I was paralyzed and remembered that I couldn't hold the microphone, so she had to improvise.

"You know what?" Terra said. "I can answer that question myself. Shannon was picked because she's the only person who has been a member for nine years, and if she's queen, that adds on an extra five years. She's like my sister, even though she's my best friend's sister."

Terra didn't want anyone to know that I was paralyzed, so she immediately stopped the questions by saying, "Look at the time. Okay, if anyone has anymore questions, write it down and I will give you some answers tomorrow. Let's skate!"

Once everyone started skating, I asked Terra, "What if someone asks me to skateboard?"

Suddenly, Terra froze up and said, "I have no idea."

Unfortunately, someone heard us talking. A girl that was a little younger than me said, "I want to see you skateboard!"

"Okay," Terra said as if she misunderstood. "I was just about to go on the half pipe."

"Not you!" the girl said. "I want to see Shannon skateboard!"

"Okay," I said. "Um... I just need to think about which tricks I'm going to do. Woody, let's talk over there."

Terra pushed Woody and me behind a tree. "What am I going to do?" I asked. I had never been more nervous than at that moment.

We were all thinking for a minute and Terra couldn't stop pacing. She stopped when she tripped over a pile of a very long and skinny piece of string. That string gave me an idea.

"Woody," I said. "Tie this string around me. Actually, tie one end of the string around me and the other end to a hang glider."

"Who's going to be on the hang glider?" Woody asked.

"You are."

"Why me?"

"Well, you mentioned it."

Terra went to a nearby shop that had hang glider rentals. "We have to make this quick," Terra said. "These hang glider rentals are by the hour and one hour is all I can afford."

"It'll be quick," I said. "I just have to do a few of my best tricks in front of the people, and then blend in to the crowd for the rest of the afternoon."

Terra got Woody in the hang glider and tied the end of the string to him and the other end of the string to me.

"Are you ready, Woody?" Terra asked. Woody nodded. "How about you?" she asked me.

"I'm ready," I said, and I was definitely ready.

Terra said to everyone, "I know it's been a while since you've seen Shannon skateboarding, due to the construction, but now she's ready." That was the signal for Woody to take off. Once Woody took off, I started moving without letting people know the truth. All I had to do was to smile at the crowd. Woody helped me flip, jump over tables, and do hand stands. He also helped me to skateboard on a wall. But when I was on the wall, my skateboard came off of my shoes and the string came loose. This made me look like I messed up, but it wasn't anyone's fault.

I fell to the ground, and everyone started to crowd around me. Even a poodle came up to me and licked my nose. This moment was the most embarrassing time of my life. I would have rather allowed everyone to know that I was paralyzed than to let them think I messed up.

Suddenly, a geek, who shouldn't have been in the skate park, came out of the crowd with a video camera. He said, "Hey, everyone! I can show you what really happened." He hooked up his video camera to a bigger screen. "As you can see here, Shannon looks like a stiff board. I only have one logical reason for this. Shannon's paralyzed!"

The entire audience started booing at me. I knew I had to leave, so I did. After I got up and took a few steps, everyone gasped and I suddenly realized that I was able to walk. The fall probably shocked my nerves. I had to show everyone my newest trick, so I picked up my skateboard and ran to the ramp. Everyone started applauding again, but there was an ambulance behind the skate park the entire time. Some doctors came out and put me in the ambulance. During the entire ride to the hospital, I said, "I'm fine! I'm fine! Let me go!" Even though I was saying that, the doctors weren't listening.

CHAPTER 10:

No, not Woody!

"Look at me!" I said to the doctors. "I'm able to walk! When I fell down, my nerves were shocked or something! I know it probably doesn't sound real to you, but it's true! I'm proof that it's true! I don't need to be here, so let me go home!" I could tell that the doctors weren't paying attention to what I was saying. They just continued doing what they were doing as if I wasn't even talking to them.

I had to stop yelling at the doctors because Kelly, Terra, Chelsea, and my mom came in my room. It wouldn't have been a good impression if they were to see me standing in the middle of the room yelling and I knew that Woody wouldn't have liked it if I was yelling. I was glad that the people closest to me all came again to see me, but I noticed that Woody wasn't there. "Wait," I said, "where's Woody? Why isn't he here? He's supposed to be here next to me."

"Shannon," Terra said, "there's something I have to tell you. After you left the skate park, Woody was having trouble getting out of the hang glider. I thought he would be okay since he landed on a nearby building. At first, it looked really funny to see him struggling, but when he got out of the hang glider, he tripped, and he fell down a three story building and landed on his leg on a table. I waited with him until the ambulance came. I couldn't get in the ambulance, so I had to wait for your mom to pick me up. We just saw Woody a minute ago, and the doctors say that he's paralyzed from the waist down. He also caught terrible bacteria when his leg cracked open on the table, and the bacteria have been spreading through him. He can't have contact with people or anything because it's very contagious, and well, to make it even worse, you'll never be able to kiss him again."

I was just speechless. All that I was able to do was to stand there and stare at Terra. Suddenly, I started to scream at the top of my lungs. After I screamed, I had to change the subject to get my mind off of it. "Will I be able to go back to school on Monday?" I said that as if I didn't hear the news about Woody, but on the inside I was still very shocked by the news. I didn't know how I was able to move on to talk about school.

"Yes," my mom replied. "Woody and Kelly will both be going to school on Monday as well, even though they're both in wheelchairs."

"Doesn't Woody need to get testing done?"

"His testing was much easier, so he finished early. The doctors just need to take a sample of the bacteria to find out what kind of bacteria it is, and Woody can go to school in an antibacterial suit."

"Where's Woody?" I just wanted her to answer my question, which was why I started to sound a little angry.

"He's down the hall in room forty-six. It's on the right side of the hall. You can't miss it."

"I'll go see how he's doing." As I walked out of my room, I noticed that Kelly made a sign that said "Shannon Bauber's room" and she also made a sign for her room and for Woody's room. I walked over to his room where he was in his wheelchair.

"What's that thing on your face?" I asked even though I wanted to say something nicer.

"This is a mask so no one catches my bacteria. This mask used to be clear and see-through, but it attracts the bacteria easily, so now it's green and see-through," he replied.

"What kind of bacteria is it?"

"The doctors don't know yet. If it turns out to be newly discovered bacteria, they might name it after me."

"That sounds interesting. I know I've always wanted something named after me, and when we were ten, you told me that you wanted something named after to be you."

"I did, but I wanted it to be something cool, like a meteor that's named after me. I didn't want it to be bacteria."

"I see what you mean, but more importantly, I heard that I can't kiss you anymore. Is that true? Was the kiss at the skate park our last kiss?"

"Yeah, but I can still give you an air kiss. Can you still kind of see my eyes?"

"I like air kisses, and I can see your eyes."

"But there's something I have to tell you."

"What?"

"The reason why the string came loose is because I got distracted by this cute little dog. My hand slipped in a way that it untied the string."

I couldn't believe that one dog caused so much trouble "I hope I never see that dog again. Anyway, I'll see you in the morning on Monday. Are you still carpooling with us?"

"Yeah, I am, I just didn't know that you'd be going back to regular school on Monday."

"You don't sound so good. What's wrong with me going back to school on Monday? I know I don't have to make up any work. I've been going to hospital school everyday for the past week Oh, did the cafeteria food turn bad, because I can start bringing my own lunch. C'mon Woody, tell me. Wait a minute, did you get a bully?"

"I didn't get a bully, but you're getting closer. Here's the hint: it's something about you."

"So what's wrong with me?"

"Oh, uh... nothing's wrong with you. So, I'll see you tomorrow, probably in the afternoon." Then he directed me to the door, and by directed, I mean pushed. "Just try to be prepared. Actually, never mind. Everything is okay, just stay near me at school, and try to be prepared."

"Hey, I know that something's wrong. What do I need to be prepared for?"

"You'll find out at school. We can talk about more tomorrow."

I could tell that he didn't want to answer my question because he closed the door on my face, and I knew that he wouldn't tell me the next day.

CHAPTER II:

There's a New Kid

Monday came and I still had no clue what Woody meant. He said that I needed to be prepared, but I didn't know what I needed to be prepared for.

"Are you ready?" Chelsea asked since she always drives Kelly and me to school every morning and she picks us up every afternoon. Sometimes she was late because of detention.

"Yeah," I said.

"So am I," Kelly said.

"Okay," Chelsea said. "Terra and Woody should be here any minute, and then we can leave for school."

Chelsea had to carpool because my mom, Woody's parents, and Terra's parents all had to go to work early and overtime. That meant that we had to leave home early and we just ate breakfast at school.

The doorbell rang. It was Terra and Woody. That meant that we were ready to go.

"Is everyone buckled in? Chelsea asked. Ever since the car crash, she had been very cautious when she had to drive. I didn't blame her because I kind of felt the same way.

After driving for ten minutes, we made it to the elementary school to drop off Kelly. After another ten minutes, Woody and I were at the junior high. Ten minutes later, Chelsea and Terra were at the high school.

At school, I didn't mind carrying Woody's books for him. He wasn't able to touch anything unless he was wearing sanitation gloves.

"Woody," I said as we were walking to class, "We're a couple, which means that we should be able to tell each other anything, and right now, I want you to tell me the truth. What do I need to be prepared for?"

"Okay," Woody said. "There's this new kid, like a bully. Her name is Gretchen Shlomp and she's after you."

"I know Gretchen Shlomp! Remember that summer when I went to camp? Gretchen was a clean freak. She wouldn't eat her dessert whenever her it touched the tray instead of her napkin, So, I take advantage of her. I always sat next to her and I would purposely move the dessert so she would give it to me. I think that she found out, but she was so nerdy."

"Well, she isn't nerdy anymore and she remembers you."

"How could she remember me? We were only eight."

"Well, she has one of our classes and I told her who I was and that I was dating you. Your name must have sounded familiar."

"Why did you tell her name in the first place?"

"She looked new and I always make sure that everyone knows about us."

"She was probably thinking about someone else with my name." That was a lie. I felt a little better if I was in denial. "Well, Shannon Bauber is a very common name."

"What if she sees you in class? You'll be dead."

"I have a plan. At ten, let's both ask for the hall pass, but I'll ask a little earlier so the teacher doesn't get suspicious."

We had to end our conversation because the bell rang. Once we were in class, I passed a note to Woody saying, "I'll tell you the rest of the plan at ten."

I was able to tell him a little more about the plan during passing period. The good thing was that those two hours went by quickly.

"Can I go to the bathroom?" I asked the teacher. As usual, the teacher said yes.

"Can I go to the bathroom?" Woody asked a few minutes later. The only way that I knew that was because I was on the other side of the door.

Once Woody left the room, I said to him, "Okay, Gretchen can't pound on me if she can't see me. So, I'm going to pass out in a minute. I'll just fake it. Then, you'll just happen to pass by and you'll carry me to the nurse's office. The nurse will call my mom and I'll go home. Once I get home, I'll make my mom think I caught your bacteria and I'll go to the hospital. I know this cool doctor who will go with my plan to dress up as someone else and my mom will think I'm stuck in the hospital again. I'll then hack into the school's files, I'll transfer to another school, and I'll be a new exchange student from some foreign country. My new name is Esha Glunposc. I'll pass out now." I was able to pass out perfectly.

Woody followed the plan exactly. He lifted me up and took me to the nurse's office. He just had to go through the front door.

"Oh my," the nurse said. "What happened?"

"I don't know," Woody said. "I just found her lying on the floor. I think she caught my bacteria." He could have made it sound more convincing. I heard some of his nervous lying voice.

"Of course, Woody, you need better sanitation gloves. The bacteria can easily come through. Oh, and I will call Shannon's mother."

The plan was going great. The nurse did call my mom. Once my mom came to school, she took me to the hospital. At the hospital, I snuck away and I met up with the cool doctor and he went with my plan.

"I need foreign clothes that will cover my face, my hair, and my skin. If you can, get me some high heels." I told him. "A different height should throw her off."

By the next day, I woke up in my hospital bed and I put on my new clothes and I became Esha Glunposc. I spent the morning practicing my new accent. Chelsea picked me up, so I had to tell her the plan.

"You kids are so stupid," Chelsea said with a laugh. "But I don't mind if I get you in trouble. But, I do want to see how would end."

"So you won't tell Mom?" I asked in my new foreign accent.

"No."

"Wait, can you do a small favor for me?"

"Oh, come on! I have to do two things for you. I rarely ever do one thing for you, but okay, what is it?"

"I need you to bring some boxes of things so I don't get bored at the hospital. You know, like my cell phone, good snacks, my music, my clothes, my savings, and movies and my DVD player"

Okay, I can do that."

"Thanks."

The carpool was exactly the same as Monday. That meant that Kelly and Terra also found out. The good thing was that they promised not to tell anyone else. This secret became known as the Car Secret.

Once Woody and I got to school, I was actually very confident. Esha was very different from Shannon. Esha was taller, had dark brown hair like Woody, and all of her skin was covered as part of a religion.

Gretchen, Woody, and I all had third period together and I knew that Gretchen thought that I transferred. Gretchen also thought that Esha was a different person, but she was a little suspicious.

She looked different than I last remembered her. She wasn't a small weak nerd like she was five years before. She turned into a giant evil monster with a rude and angry look on her face.

"Where's that girlfriend of yours?" Gretchen asked Woody.

"We had an argument and we broke up," Woody lied perfectly, without the nervous lying voice. He must have been practicing. "She didn't want to see me again so she transferred to a different school in a different city."

"So does that mean you're available? If you are, I don't mind being your girlfriend." That was a lie. Gretchen somehow found out about part of the plan. I just hoped that she didn't know I was Esha.

"Well, I'm not ready to start dating again." His lie really saved himself and possibly saved me, but he started to sound scared. I didn't blame him for being scared because I was also getting scared.

"When you do start dating, can I be your girlfriend then?"

"No!" I said with my foreign accent. I really just wanted to say that in my head, so I knew I had to say something else. So, I continued. "I mean Woody has a deadly bacteria and he can't make physical contact with anyone."

"Right," Woody said, really sounding scared. "Thanks Esha. I wouldn't be able to hug or kiss you."

"Well, can I stop by your house?" Gretchen asked. "But if you aren't there, I'll be very mad."

I wasn't able to let Woody give his address to Gretchen, so I lied again. I got in front of her, patted her shoulder, and said, "Woody won't be home. He'll be staying at the hospital in room one."

"Okay," Gretchen said as she wrote that on a piece of paper. "I'll see you sometime. I want to make my visits a surprise, so you won't know when you'll see me."

I could have sworn Gretchen gave an evil laugh as she went to her seat. She was definitely on to our plan. The conversation ended when the bell rang.

After school, I talked to Woody. I said, "This is really bad, Woody. What if Gretchen tells everyone that we broke up?"

"First of all, I broke up with Shannon Bauber, not Esha," Woody said. "Second, the real problem is that I'll be surprised by Gretchen anytime, and I really don't want to be surprised."

"You don't have to worry about that. I sneaked a tracker on Gretchen during class. My cell phone will beep when Gretchen is one mile away from us, so we have to go to the hospital as soon as possible because Chelsea probably just dropped off the boxes. One mile will give me enough time to sneak away because I won't spend my entire day in foreign clothes."

"But how will that help me?"

"Well, as soon as my phone starts to beep, we can get to room one, lock the door, and I'll play sound effects as if you're in surgery. Maybe I can impersonate a doctor to make it sound more realistic.

"But how do I convince my parents to let me stay in the hospital?"

"Tell them that the nurses want to supervise your bacteria more closely."

Woody did call his parents, but he had sanitation wipes all over his cell phone. He finished the call right when Chelsea came.

"Sorry I'm late," Chelsea said. "I got detention for some reason that I don't know of."

"Chelsea," I said. "Can you drop off Woody at the hospital with me? His parents are okay with."

"Okay, and I played hooky for the morning so I could pack your boxes. They're in the trunk."

"Maybe that's why you got detention." When I opened the trunk, the boxes were there with everything I needed, including my cell phone, so I put my cell phone in my backpack.

After ten minutes, we made it to the hospital. "Woody," I said. "I'll go back to my room to change and I'll let you know when Gretchen is near. But in the meantime, I'm going to skateboard so I don't get bored, and you can do your homework."

"Okay," Woody said.

After ten minutes, I changed into my regular clothes and I ran out the hospital entrance. Since the parking lot in front of the hospital was completely empty, it was a perfect place to bring out benches to jump over. I knew about a skateboard ramp that was in a nearby alley that I brought to the parking lot.

Unfortunately, I forgot to take my cell phone out of my backpack which was in my room, and it must have started to beep.

Gretchen came by on her bike to the hospital about ten minutes later. I felt sorry for that poor bike. She said, "Well, well, well. I thought you two broke up."

"We did, but... um ... I... um," I couldn't think of any lie that would work.

"Oh, please, ever since I came to this school, I knew you two were lying to me all along. Woody, you broke your promise. Now I'm going to break you."

"But my bacteria is real," Woody said.

"Okay then," she said while she made her hands into fists. "Then I won't break you. I'll break your girlfriend instead. Come with me Shannon."

Gretchen was a real bully. She actually punched me in my face and in my gut. She even pushed me against the wall several times. Then, she shoved me in a dumpster. She knew that the garbage truck was coming soon, and it did.

For two hours, I was in the garbage truck and I eventually was taken to the dump. Luckily, a garbage man saved from being in a landfill. I got a ride to the public showers then I walked to the hospital. I got checked for fractured or broken bones. Luckily, I just had a lot of bruises. The best part was that my mom never knew about it.

CHAPTER 12:

Hey, You're better!

"Do you know how scared I feel hen I'm around Gretchen now?" I said while I was safe in my hospital room. "She probably came to our school after getting expelled for murdering someone."

"You know that could be the reason. What will you do when your mom sees you with all these bruises?" Woody asked. "She'll probably sew the hospital because she'll think it's their fault."

"Easy, I can cover up the bruises with make-up and cover up. The only problem is that I don't have enough cover up and I don't want to waste my make-up. So, I'll change into my foreign clothes and skateboard to the pharmacy."

"Okay, I'll be in my room, but don't be too late."

"Why?"

"At five thirty, I'm going to get my first treatment for the bacteria, and I want you to be there to keep me company."

"Relax. The pharmacy isn't far from here, and I'm only getting cover up."

"Okay, but it's already five."

"Okay, then get out of my way so I can leave."

I started walking to the front door when I realized that I forgot something. I went back to my room and grabbed my skateboard and some money from my savings. Then, I ran back outside and I skateboarded to the pharmacy.

I was able to make it to the pharmacy in less than ten minutes. The pharmacy was small, so I was able to find the cover up I was looking for. Since the bottles of cover up were also small, I grabbed a lot of them, and I had to enough money.

On my way out of the pharmacy, I noticed a mirror. Even though I was bruised, my face still looked great. My blond hair was fine, too. Then it hit me. I wasn't wearing my disguise. My entire face was showing and I was standing out in public wearing plain American clothes. I got back on my skateboard and I quickly went back to the hospital. I was hoping that Gretchen wasn't around to see me. Luckily, she didn't.

Once I got back to the hospital, Woody said, "I'm so glad you came back in one piece! You forgot your disguise!"

"I know," I said. "Well, at least I'm back before your treatment. By the way, what's your treatment?"

"I'm going to sit in a room drinking every antibiotic while being sprayed by every bacteria-killing disinfectant."

"Isn't that dangerous?"

"I'm going to be supervised by nurses and doctors."

"Okay, your treatment should begin-"

"Woody Parker," a nurse said. "It's time for your treatment."

"Now," I finished.

I went with the nurse and Woody to this room that I never knew about because I had never seen any floor beyond the first floor. This room was on the third floor in room 301. On the ceiling of this room, there were disinfectants hanging. There was a specialized chair that was covered in disinfectants where Woody was sitting. One wall was replaced with glass so doctors and nurses and I would watch Woody to make sure nothing went wrong.

A doctor counted down, "Three, two, one, go."

The antibiotics traveled from a tube that was leading to Woody's mouth. He was wearing goggles so the disinfectants wouldn't get in his eyes.

"Has this ever been done before?" I asked one of the doctors.

"No," the doctor responded. "This room was started being built when Woody was diagnosed."

That answer wasn't making me feel any better. I then asked, "Then how do you know this is going to work?"

"We don't," the doctor said. "Woody will either come out of the room free of the bacteria, or he'll have the outcome of death."

"I want him out of that room!" I yelled. I just couldn't stand there watching my boyfriend risk death. I ran to the door and I went in. I had to shield my eyes so I wouldn't get sprayed by the disinfectants. I was aware that the doctors ran after me trying to get me out of the room, and I was now risking death, but I still got Woody out of the chair. I forgot that he was paralyzed, so he was dragged out of the room.

"I'm sorry I have to drag you," I said as I was running.

"It's okay," Woody said. "I'm running."

"I can't believe you're running. I should let go of your hand so I don't get your bacteria."

"If I still had my bacteria, you would have gotten it by now. I think I'm better now."

Since the doctors weren't chasing us anymore, we stopped running.

"Woody, do you realize that you're now vulnerable to Gretchen?"

"What do you mean?"

"Gretchen didn't beat you up earlier today because you were sick. You need to come to school in your wheelchair and wearing that mask."

"What'll happen to you?"

"Gretchen still doesn't know that I'm disguised as Esha. As far as I'm concerned, we can be in disguise for as long as we want."

"But what am I supposed to say to my parents when I get home in a wheelchair? I don't think that I can go back to the hospital. The doctors think I'm okay."

I spent a few moments thinking, and then I said, "Tell your parents that you're tutoring me after school, that way you can stay at my house for a few hours and you can leave your wheelchair in Chelsea's car. Then, you'll walk home and Chelsea will take me to the hospital."

It was getting a little late, so I called Chelsea to come and pick us up. I didn't have my cell phone with me, but I did have some money left to use a payphone. While we were waiting, I realized that I had my bag of cover up in my hand the whole time. I decided to apply it so Chelsea wouldn't asked questions. I knew that if she found out, she would have held it against me.

CHAPTER 13:

School Paper

Once Woody and I got home, I told Chelsea about my plan, but I wasn't sure if she even needed to know about my plan. "You've got to be kidding me!" Chelsea laughed at the thought of another one of my plans. Then, I knew that I didn't need to tell her the plan. "You've been making up these dumb plans since you were paralyzed. Actually, the first dumb plan was the suitcase, and be lucky that I forgave you for it. For your sake, I'll be the nice big sister again and I won't tell Mom. This will go along with the Car Secret. So, in the car tomorrow, I'll also make sure to tell Kelly to stay quiet about it."

"For some reason you have been really nice to me about my plans," I said. "You want something. You always do this. What do you want this time? What, do you want my money?"

"Actually, that's exactly what I was thinking. I wouldn't mind having a month of your allowance. But since your allowance is smaller than mine, I'll take two months."

"Okay." I knew that it was a bit of a sacrifice, but it was worth less than letting my mom know.

Wait a minute. I think I'll take three months of your allowance."

"Why? That's kind of pushing it."

"Maybe to you it is, but not to me. I've been going along with three different dumb plans. One month for each plan. I just think it's fair."

"There haven't been three plans."

"Yeah, first there was the suitcase, then the ditching, and now the disguise."

"Okay." I knew that that had to be my last plan to tell Chelsea about. I didn't want her to take more of my money. I only had my savings left.

"So the deal is made."

On the next day, Chelsea told Kelly and Terra about the plan, and how it's part of the Car Secret. They both promised not to tell anyone. At school, Woody and I had the same disguises on as yesterday. There was something very different though. Every person who passed by me said, "How's it going, Esha?" I was okay with it at first because I thought those people heard about a foreign exchange student, but then more people started to say that. I knew that something was out of the ordinary. It didn't matter if the person was a popular friend of mine or a complete nerd. I felt like my life was about to come to an end.

I ran to Woody and pulled the collar of his shirt and said, "What happened?!"

Woody pulled my hands of his shirt and calmly said with a normal voice, "Someone found out that you were Esha Glunposc instead of Shannon Bauber to avoid being bullied."

"Who did this?" I was really panicking about it.

"I believe that would be me," Gretchen was standing right behind me with an evil grin on her face. I didn't even have to turn around to know it was her. Her shadow was enough to block the sun.

"Why?" I asked.

"I wanted to ruin your life, duh?" Gretchen said. "I know how you don't want me to bully you, so I thought I would stop and let someone else have a chance."

"I meant why me?"

"I don't know many people here, and I got to know you for an entire summer." She literally picked me up by my shirt and threw me to the hard cement floor.

"How did you even get to write an article in the paper?" Woody asked as he tried to hide behind me when I got up, which was hard because he was taller than me.

"Easy," Gretchen said. "Anyone part of the school news press can write an article. Oh, and if you read my article, you'll know that students can win prizes if they find you and punch you when I'm around. So, you better watch your back."

"Don't worry, Shannon, I'll watch your back," Woody said.

"I don't think so," she said. "Students are after you too, and if you were smart, you won't be a snitch. Isn't it great that the teachers don't read the school news paper?"

Suddenly, I wanted to scream. I said, "This was supposed to be an ordinary day, and you ruined it! You ruined my life! Because of you, everyone at this school forgot that Woody and I are the most popular couple! This is all your fault! If you never came here, I wouldn't have hidden all the time, or watched my back, or lied to my own mom! I set the worst influence on my little sister! I know you don't think I'm the fighting type, but what do you think of me now?!"

The bell rang, and I started a fight, which I had never done before, and it was the first fight to ever occur at that junior high. I knew that I was supposed to go to class with the others, but instead I started punching Gretchen in the face and everyone in the school stayed to watch the fight. I knew I had to do something, that's why the other students were saying, "Fight, fight, fight!" My wig came off when I started punching Gretchen. Everyone gasped and started to cheer for either me or for Gretchen. There was an affect, but Gretchen just punched me back. I was surprised that the fight was five minutes long. It ended when the principal stepped in after I got a black eye. We were all silent and stopped what we were doing.

He said, "Fight's over! Everyone get to class. Shlomp, Bauber, come with me." Gretchen and I followed the principal to the nurse's office. He gave us a lecture about why fighting is wrong while the nurse applied bandages on Gretchen and me. The nurse also took our x-rays to check for broken bones. Luckily, there were none, but my clothes were stained with blood.

CHAPTER 14:

It's my Fault

I was sitting on the bed in the nurse's office with Gretchen. When the nurse left the room, I turned to Gretchen and I said, "When I said that it was your fault, I didn't mean it. I was just so mad that I couldn't control myself. I'm sorry for what's happened. I know now that I shouldn't blame you for being a bully."

"Well," Gretchen said, "I don't think there's anyone to blame here, unless, we both want to blame each other, but that's probably a really bad idea."

"Well, I don't feel like blaming you anymore. I mean, at first I did, but not anymore. That's not exactly true when you say that there's no one to blame. It's my fault, not yours. I won't blame you, but it's okay if you want to blame me. If I wasn't pretending to be someone else, I wouldn't be in the school news paper. If I faced my fears, I wouldn't have pretended to be someone else. If you and I go back to when we were eight at summer camp, I would have changed the fact that I took advantage of you. If I was nicer, I wouldn't be in this giant mess."

"Don't forget about Woody. If you were nicer, he wouldn't be paralyzed nor have that gross bacteria."

"Yeah, I wish that none of this ever happened and that I can turn back time, so no one will remember that any of this happened. I need to say it again. I'm sorry. I used to think that if I was in trouble, I could get out by lying."

"You don't have to keep apologizing. Maybe it's not too late to turn things around. I can't turn back time or make people forget about it, and wishing probably isn't going to help us now. But, I think there's something else that we can do. You could be right about lying. It might help us now."

"I'm in too deep. What are we going to do? How's lying going to help us?"

"If you got in the mess by lying, you can get out with lying. I'll stop picking on you and I'll write a special edition of the newspaper today to tell everyone that the hurting is officially over. I can get everyone to know by the end of the day. Then, you'll be safe."

"That sounds like a good idea. But how will we write a newspaper in such short notice?"

"I have my sources. If you want you can help too."

Gretchen and I went to the classroom where the school news press is at, even though we should have been in our first period class at that time. The classroom was a complete mess, but it was probably because people worked really hard to make a good news paper. We didn't want to waste the paper, so we sent it to everyone's cell phone. We had to keep the message short, since we had to use our own cell phones. The message said, "Gretchen Shlomp is moving and going to another school. The prize no longer exists. Leave Woody Parker and Shannon Bauber alone and don't harm them in anyway."

Then, we hooked up our cell phone to the school directory on the computer, and the message was sent. Once we sent the message, I was able to go out into the world freely and live my life again. When the massages were sent, I heard a lot of cell phones.

"This is great," I said. "Now everyone will love me again. I'm going to be as popular as ever, and so is Woody, and it's all thanks to you." I gave her a big hug, but she just pushed me away.

"It's been great going to this school, and I've had a good time, but I think that this may be the last time that I'll ever see you. The last seven days at this school have been really great, but I have to leave."

"What do you mean? Why is this the last time I'll see you? Why do you have to leave? Stay here, we finally just became friends."

"I came here after bullying a kid who took advantage of me during another year of camp. I got expel for fighting, and that's probably going to happen again. I know we both have detention for a week, but I'll tell the principal that's I started the fight. I'll make sure that I transfer to a school outside the district where I don't know anyone from the past. I can't help it that I have rage issues."

"I'm going to miss you. This has been great. I'm glad that we did this, and I'm glad we were able to fix everything."

"Great, but what's your mom going to think when she finds out that you faked a serious illness? What are Woody's parents going to think when they find out that he was lying about paralysis? You two are in big trouble. Then again, so am I. I know that I'm getting expelled."

"I have another plan, again, but this is only going to help me. I'll tell my mom about the lies when she's at her happiest, and I'm pretty sure that happens when she's with her friends at the annual special weekend. The only way I can do that is to sneak into the rental bus. That means I'll need some help. Last year, my sister Chelsea drove the bus, so I think that she'll probably drive the bus again this year. I can stow away in her suitcase and I'll sit in the back of the bus where no one would notice me. When they least expect it, I'll pop out and tell her everything. It's perfect!" I stood up with pride and a smile on my face. I had confidence that I could go through with the plan and end it with success. All I had to do was to come up with the small details.

CHAPTER 15:

Special Weekend

Once I got home, I told Chelsea about my plan and to tell mom to move up the special weekend to the upcoming weekend. I forgot about my allowance, so she took another month. The special weekend consisted of a picnic, a spa day, and a beauty pageant and it only happened once a year. They've been having the special weekend ever since they graduated from college.

"Hi Mom," Chelsea said on the phone.

"Chelsea," Mom said, "office jobs are a lot of hard work. I told you not to call me, so make it quick." She had always gotten angry to get a phone call at work.

"Okay," Chelsea said. "So I was thinking about moving up your special weekend to this weekend."

"That's a great idea." Then, she started to cheer up. "There are a few conditions though. You're driving the bus, you will set up the bus rental, you will hire the babysitter for Shannon and Kelly, and you will need to call my friends."

"Got it, I already started." She said that because she already started looking for the friends' phone numbers. My mom had seven different friends. Chelsea was able to call all of them and they all were able to make it.

Kelly said that she was able to sleep over at a friend's house for the weekend, so Chelsea didn't have to bother to call a babysitter, but Kelly really wanted to be a part of the special weekend. I only packed the necessities, so I could fit in Chelsea's suitcase.

Saturday morning came by fast because Chelsea and I had to wake up at five in the morning. Chelsea was able to pick up the bus and I was able to get myself fitted in the suitcase before my mom woke up and her friends arrived. Terra also came in case Chelsea couldn't drive for some reason.

"I can't believe I'm giving up an entire weekend of skateboarding to be in some ladies' day," Terra complained.

"You know that you can skateboard during the picnic," Chelsea said.

"Okay. I'll grab my skateboard. I left it in your house next to Shannon's." Terra went inside and came out with a skateboard. Then she said, "Where's Shannon's skateboard?"

"Shannon is sneaking on the bus. She wants to tell my mom some bad news when she's at her happiest."

When I was in the back of the bus, Chelsea threw all the other suitcases at me. Luckily, I was able to make my way out of the suitcase. I noticed two other suitcases moving around. My first thought was that someone brought pets. Then I knew that they weren't pets. The zipper started to move, and out came Kelly.

"What are you doing here?" I whispered.

"I lied about the sleepover," Kelly replied, "and I really wanted to come. So, I followed the same plan that you and Woody did."

"I didn't want Woody to come!" I started to whisper a little louder.

"Well, he's here and he's in that moving suitcase." Kelly was right. The zipper started to move on the moving suitcase. Woody came out.

"Hey Shannon," Woody said, also whispering. "Why didn't you tell me the plan yourself instead of Kelly?"

"Because my plan only involved me," I said. "We should stop talking or else everyone will know we're here."

"What was that noise?" my mom asked.

"Um...it was the motor," Chelsea lied. "Yeah, this bus is one of the older versions, and it's been used a lot for long trips. I would've picked another one, but this was the only one available. It was this or a minivan." All the woman thought that sounded reasonable. Chelsea continued. "I need to check to make sure that all the suitcases are okay. I don't want any beaten up luggage."

She then signaled Terra to take the wheel so she was able to get up. When she got to the back of the bus, she looked at me and whispered, "You guys better shut up and stay still. Everyone might be getting suspicious."

"Chelsea, are you talking to yourself?" my mom asked. "You don't usually do that."

"I'm not talking to myself, really," Chelsea said. "I was just thinking out loud about which way I should which way I should drive. I just want us to be at the park early so we find a good parking spot."

"If you want to get us there early, why don't you read these directions?" my mom said as she handed Chelsea the piece of paper.

"Yeah, earlier so I can skateboard," Terra murmured as she switched seats with Chelsea. Then in a louder voice, she said, "So Mrs. B. is this park near a skateboard allowed area?"

"Of course not," my mom said. "This park is very formal with no young children. You're here with Chelsea because you two are acting very lady-like these past few years. Maybe in a few more years Shannon will come with us. It's a shame that you couldn't make it last year."

"You lied to me about the skating," Terra said to Chelsea.

"Sorry, I forgot," Chelsea replied.

Chelsea continued to drive for another hour. We did get to the park at an early hour and the park was completely empty. Terra and Chelsea checked on Woody, Kelly, and me.

"I need to get out of this suitcase now!" I said.

"It's a little too early for everyone to recognize you. Mom isn't at her happiest yet and they probably remember you guys from last year," Chelsea said as she pulled me out of her suitcase.

"I know," I said. "I'll stand on Woody's shoulders and we'll put on a dress. I'll wear a big hat with sunglasses and Woody will wear high heels."

"That's a good plan, except the part about me wearing high heels," Woody said as he got out of the suitcase. "But were will we find those things?"

"We'll have to borrow," I said as I pulled out a dress. Kelly went along with the plan and pulled out the accessories. She also pulled out a big shirt, a smaller hat, smaller sunglasses, and smaller shoes.

"What are you doing?" I asked Kelly.

"I'll disguise myself to look like a small woman," Kelly replied. "You're not the only sneaky one in the family."

Kelly and I went to the park bathroom to change. Woody stayed outside to put on the high heels. Once I came out of the bathroom, I got on Woody to sit on his shoulders. Kelly and I worked on our voices to sound like ladies while we followed Terra and Chelsea to the ladies' picnic.

"Hello, Mother," Chelsea said. "I noticed these two ladies and they were hoping to join us."

"Hello," I said in a different voice. "I am Sharon, and this is my friend Katherine. As you can see, Katherine isn't able to walk and she has laryngitis, so I will be talking for her." Kelly glared at me because she wanted to talk. I just glared back at her.

"That is perfectly fine with us," my mom said. "Why don't you take a seat on the picnic blanket?"

Sitting down was difficult to do since I was standing on Woody, and he practically tripped. Luckily, I wasn't injured, but Woody was probably a little hurt.

During the picnic, we chatted, ate fancy foods I'd never heard of, and planned out the rest of the special weekend. The picnic lasted for an hour and a half. Then, we went to the hotel for spa time.

"You two should join us," my mom said to Kelly and me.

"We would be glad to join you," I said. Right after I answered, I thought of something. Woody was under me. I thought about it when we walked in the hotel.

"Chelsea, Terra," my mom said. "Take the luggage to our hotel room. Chelsea, you know which one I'm talking about."

"Now I know why the last teenage driver left," Chelsea whispered to Terra.

I bent down to look like I was listening to Kelly, and Kelly looked like she was whispering something in my ear. Then, I said, "Excuse me ladies, Katherine and I will join you at the spa right after we visit the restroom."

Once we were out of the ladies' sight, I told Woody, "I have a plan."

"Oh, what a surprise," he said angrily. "I'm sorry, but I can't stand to be in your plans anymore. As soon as Kelly asked me to come, I should have said no. I can't live like this anymore! It's over between us!"

I couldn't believe that he even said that. I just acted as if he never said that and I kissed him for about ten seconds and then said, "Now, what were you saying?"

"Nothing, except that I'll go along with the plan and you are the only girl for me."

"That's what I thought. As I was saying, I'll tell the ladies I want to spend all day in a mud bath. If I'm in the mud bath, no one can see my feet. You will be under my towel, and when I get in, you will swim to the surface. Ask for a towel for your hair and cucumber slices for your eyes. I'll do the same thing."

This plan went perfectly, just like my other plans. All the ladies did other spa activities without Kelly and me. After staying in the mud for about two hours, my skin was at its softest.

After we left the spa, we went straight to the hotel room. We didn't do much in the hotel room except talk about the beauty pageant and watch soap operas. Everything was very boring until my mom ordered the snack bar to our room. I didn't usually overstuff, but this wasn't an ordinary day. Luckily, I remembered about Woody. I filled a bag with various foods and gave it to Woody when no one was looking. No one heard Woody eating because they were so loud crying while watching romance movies.

In the morning, all the ladies rushed to there other special hotel room, which was where the beauty pageant took place. Last year, Chelsea told me, "The beauty pageant is very short. They put on their dresses. They go on stage. They get off the stage. This is repeated for the talent and the swimsuits. Then, they're all winners. It was only like half an hour."

The pageant was exactly like how Chelsea said. Kelly, Chelsea, Terra, and I weren't in the pageant. We just applauded.

Right after the pageant when everyone was a winner, and my mom was at her happiest, I told my mom in my normal voice, "I'm not Sharon. I'm your daughter Shannon and this is Kelly." I took off the dress and jumped off of Woody as Kelly took off her disguise. "I lied to you. I never got sick with Woody's bacteria. Woody doesn't even have the bacteria anymore and he can walk. I pretended to be sick so I didn't have to go to school or see that bully who beat me up twice. I'm sorry."

I saw the sadness in her eyes. I didn't want to tell her all that, but I knew that telling her would clear my conscience. I thought it would make me feel better if I told her, but I felt even worse than when I was lying.

I grabbed Woody's hand and we ran to a bus stop. I had enough money with me to pay for all three of us. We were all quiet the whole bus ride, which was over two hours long.

CHAPTER 16:

Busted!

As we got off the bus, I saw a police car coming into the driveway. The siren was on, so I instantly knew that something was wrong.

"Why are the police here?" Woody asked in a whisper. I could tell that Woody was scared.

"How should I know," I said, and I was as scared as Woody. "Maybe we should get in through the back." We started walking around the house, but then the officer came out of the car and asked, "Do any of you know Shannon Bauber?"

"No, officer," I said in an innocent voice. I couldn't believe that I just lied to a police officer. It was so common for me to lie that I didn't realize who I was lying to. Woody and Kelly both looked at me wondering why I lied.

The officer shined a light at the three of us, and then she kept the light on me as she pulled out a piece of paper. When I saw the paper, I knew at that moment that I was looking at my mug shot.

Since I had never been to jail before, the picture was just my recent school picture.

Then she said, "You're coming with me. You kids need a ride home?"

"No," Kelly and Woody said at the same time. I threw the house key to Woody and he quickly pushed Kelly home.

The officer put handcuffs on me, pushed me in the backseat of the police car, and shut the door. Then, she got in the drivers seat and took me to jail. I looked toward Woody as he ran and I mouthed out the words "help me," hoping that he would turn back and actually help me.

Even though I was scared, after a few minutes, I still had the guts to asked, "Why am I going to jail?"

"You know why," she said. "You impersonated a foreign exchange student, which is fraud, and that's against the law."

"But how did you know it was fraud? Foreign exchange students come to the country all the time."

"You hacked into the school files. We caught you when you transferred out from your old school, you didn't say which school you were transferring into. Also, when you entered Esha Glunposc into the school, you said that she was from Ukislovia."

"So?"

"That's not a real country."

"Well... um... I said that I was in the hospital."

"Yes, but your mother had checked you out of the hospital already."

I was quiet for the rest of the ride. I knew that lying wasn't going to help at that moment and I had nothing to defend myself. There was nothing else that I could've said to convince the officer to let me go. So, I came up with another choice. I tried to move my arms all the way around myself, but I wasn't flexible enough to do that. Then, I came up with another option. I swung my legs to the car door. My plan was to unlock the door with my feet, but that plan failed when the officer said, "You can't escape. The door will only unlock if you press this button on the front car door."

I had finally run out of lies and clever plans. All that was left to do was to stay seated and look out the window. Then, I thought of one final plan. I was going to smash the window. I pulled my legs on the seat and with all my power; I threw my head against the window. Unfortunately, that plan didn't work either. As soon as my head hit the window, I fell to my back and my head was in throbbing pain. I would have thought of other plans, but I was already at the police station and my head hurt too much to think.

The officer opened the car door and pulled me out. I was forced into a room. My handcuffs were taken off. I thought that they were letting me go, but then they had me hold a card with numbers on it. Then, I was thrown into a cell.

The cell had about five other child criminals. All of them looked like they had committed crimes that were way worse than what I did. Suddenly, someone in the cell came up to me. He had a shaved head and tattoos on his arm. "Hey Shannon, you want a cigarette?" he asked me.

"No," I said, and I turned away. It freaked me out that a criminal knew my name. "How do you have cigarettes in jail?"

"I have my ways," he said

Then, I looked at him again. "You look familiar. Do I know you from somewhere?"

"You should. We used to date like a year ago."

Then it hit me I was talking to Rusty, my first boyfriend. He was the guy I dated before I dated Woody. I dumped him went he stopped calling me, and when I called him on his cell phone, the number didn't exist anymore. I had always wondered what had happened to him, and I had just found out.

"Rusty, what did you do? I mean, what are you doing here?"

"Well, I shaved my head, got some tattoos, robbed a bank, and I stole a car."

"Why?"

"My parents lost all their money and I wanted to help."

"What about your tattoos and your head?"

I thought it would be cool. So, I kidnapped this tattoo artist and I shaved my head myself."

I was shocked. I remembered him as a really nice guy and he was as innocent as I was back then. But the key words were "back then." But then I realized that I shouldn't have been blaming him so much. He stole money because his parents were going broke. I was in jail for fraud, and that was for me, not for my family.

Fortunately, I heard the words I was waiting for. The officer came to open the cell to let me out. She said, "Shannon Bauber, you may have your one phone call now."

For my only phone call, I decided to call Woody's cell phone. I would have called my home number, but I didn't want to risk having my mom answer if she was home, and Woody knew what was going on.

I dialed the number. "Hello?" Woody said. I was relieved that he answered.

"It's me, Shannon," I said. "I'm in jail."

"Yeah, I know. I was the one standing there when you got arrested. Did you find out why you're in jail?

"Yeah, I'm in jail for fraud. The police caught on to what I was doing. I think I need your lawyer."

"Why do you need my lawyer instead of your lawyer?"

"I don't want my mom to know I'm in jail."

"Okay, I'll call my lawyer right now."

"Thanks, and have your lawyer call the jail, that way I can get out of here sooner."

"Okay. Bye"

I waited in that cell for an hour until I was let out. Woody's lawyer won the case and Woody was waiting with Kelly outside of the police station. When I got out, I hugged Woody and we took a second bus ride home. Kelly had grabbed some money from home so we were able to take the bus. Even this bus ride was quiet. I was glad to finally be out of jail, but Woody looked sad. I had to ask him, "What's wrong?"

He didn't answer me. Actually, it was almost like he was ignoring me. I decided to just stay quiet on the bus and wait until we were home again.

CHAPTER 17:

What's this?

When we got of the bus at 4:00, Woody didn't go home. He knew that I didn't feel that great. Even when we were home, no one would talk. I was the first one to say something.

"How did you get me out of jail?" I asked.

"I had to pay for your bail," Woody said sadly. "I had to give up half of my life savings to get you out. But, I'm not going to hold that against you. I was the one who didn't stop you even though I knew about it. I could have also gone to jail just for knowing about it."

I was going to say something, but then the phone rang. I looked at the caller ID and noticed that Terra was calling on her cell phone. I didn't want to talk, so I handed the phone to Kelly.

"Hi Terra," Kelly said.

"Hi Kelly," Terra said. "Chelsea is taking a long time to get home because she's taking your mom to someone else's house. Chelsea and I will be home soon so you kids won't be alone."

"Okay," Kelly said, and then she hung up and told me what Terra said.

"Shannon," Woody said, "I was thinking and maybe we should bring home your stuff from the hospital since, you know, you're not going to hide there anymore. I'll go with you if you want. I can help carry some things."

Sure," I said.

The sun was close to setting when we were walking to the hospital. Once we were at the hospital, I remembered to tell the cool doctor that the plan was over. Woody was a big help to carry all my things. Being in the hospital again brought back so many bad memories. I skateboarded out of the hospital so I could get away as fast as I could.

When we were home, Chelsea and Terra were already there.

"Where should I put all this stuff?" Woody asked.

"Put it in my room," I said. "You could help me go through them. I know that there are some things I want to get rid of, like the foreign disguise."

"Hey, remember what Mom says," Chelsea yelled as I went upstairs.

"I know," I said. "I'll keep the door open."

We spent all night going through my things to see what to keep and what to give away. Woody noticed a box that seemed strange to him. He said, "What's this?"

I opened the box. I said, "Oh, these are some videos Chelsea grabbed before for me, but I she should have packed only DVD's. I decided to keep myself entertained while I was in the hospital. These are all just random movies, and there are some movies I didn't even get a chance to see." I looked through the movies to see the titles. Suddenly, I found a video that didn't have a case and had no title written on it.

"It could just be a home video from when you were a little kid," Woody said, "and your mom forgot to label it."

"I don't know. Let's go to the living room and watch it."

Terra, Chelsea, and Kelly were all in the living room doing nothing. They watched me as I came in the living room and put the video in the VCR. I turned on the TV and sat down quietly.

"What's that?" Chelsea asked.

"I don't know," I said. "I found it in a box and I want to know what it is. I think it's a home video."

"Doubt it. Mom always labeled home videos, and she didn't have time to make home videos after Dad got in the hospital."

"I still want to know want it is."

I hit the play button, and on TV, an elderly woman appeared.

"I know who that is," Chelsea said. I put it on pause. "That's Grandma. She died like nine years ago. Kelly wasn't even born and you probably kind of remember her. She was so fun when she used to baby sit us."

I hit the play button. Grandma said, "If you are watching this, that means I'm dead. This video version of my will is meant for my eldest daughter May and her daughters. May, you will receive $100,000. This money is for you and your daughters to share. I'm not mentioning your husband because I know he can't spend it if he's in the hospital with cancer. Chelsea, Shannon, and the baby who's coming, you each will receive membership the best private school in Los Angeles. I know you don't go to school yet Shannon, but when you do, you will go to the private school. Chelsea, I know how your friend Terra likes to skateboard, and I know that she's teaching Shannon to skateboard, so they will both receive a lifetime supply of skateboard gear. I hope she still likes to skateboard. Well, that's all. By the way, I suggest naming the baby Kelly, since I remember you telling me that it's a girl."

I turned off the TV since I knew that it was over. We all looked at each other. We were all happy until I said, "Why didn't Mom tell us about this? We could all be in a better home. I could've been bully-free if I went to a private school!"

"Don't look at me!" Chelsea said. "I never knew about this either! I knew that she died, but I didn't know she had a will! I was too young to know what a will was."

"I could be famous by now if I had better gear!" Terra said. "I could be more than just queen of the skate park!"

"Someone call Mom now!" Kelly said.

"Forget about calling her!" I said. "Let's get in the car and tell her in person! Someone grab the video!"

Woody got the video out of the VCR and we all ran to Chelsea's car. Chelsea drove fast without the speed being illegal. We were all at my mom's friend's house within ten minutes. When we were there, we all banged on the door as hard as we could. My mom answered quickly. "What are you kids doing here? It's nearly midnight and you all have school tomorrow."

"Forget about school, Mom!" Chelsea said as she showed her the video.

"Why didn't you tell us about Grandma's will? She gave you $100,000, Shannon and Kelly and I were supposed to be in private school, and Terra and Shannon were supposed to get skateboard gear!"

"Where did you find that?"

"It doesn't matter where we found it. Tell us why we never knew about it."

"Kids, take a seat. Did you see the part after she explained that she named Kelly?"

"It ends after that."

"It's just a long pause. After the pause, she explains that she can't possibly give all that because she's not rich. Then she says that she would give us the home we're now living in so Chelsea would be closer to Terra, we would be closer to the hospital, and we can get out of that small apartment. She also recommends that Terra should visit the new skate park, because it was close and had free membership. Now, that's the skate park that you always visit."

We were all no longer furious at her. Then, she continued. "Then she says that Shannon should meet a nice little boy her age named Woody Parker who lived next door. After that, she tells me to play in the lottery with the same numbers. As a matter of fact, someone hand me the news paper so I can check my numbers."

I handed my mom the newspaper. She compared the numbers. Her first number was right, and so was her second number, and so was her third number and fourth number, and the bonus number!

That week's lottery was for 54 million dollars. I screamed out loud, "We're rich!"

Everyone was happy. We all gave a group hug.

"Kelly," Chelsea said, "are you standing?"

We all looked at Kelly. "I'm standing! It's a miracle!"

We all started to stare at Kelly.

"Okay, I lied," she said. "I faked the paralysis so I could be in a wheelchair and get excused from gym. I was going to tell you went Shannon confessed, but she pulled me out before I could say anything."

"Let's go home," my mom said, and we completely ignored what Kelly said. "I just need to tell my friend that I'm leaving. You kids get in the car."

CHAPTER 18:

We got a Dog

Once we got home, my mom said, "Since there isn't any school tomorrow, we can do something together. I can get off from work for a day. Woody, Terra, you two can come back tomorrow morning if you want." I was glad that she wasn't working for once.

Woody and Terra walked home in the dark. We were all extremely tired at that time, especially, considering how much happened in one day. So, we all easily fell asleep that night.

In the morning when everyone was awake and in the living room, I said, "What are we going to do with our money?" We had never had so much money in our lives.

"I'm not sure," my mom said. We haven't really talked about it yet, but let's not waste it all on luxuries, but we could get a few."

"I know," Kelly said. "We should get a pet." We had never had a pet before, so we were all very excited. Before, we couldn't even afford to have a pet.

"What kind of pet?" Chelsea asked. "There are a lot of animals to choose from."

"Maybe we should get a common pet. How about a cat," I said.

"I'm allergic," Woody said.

"We should get a lizard," Terra said. "That would be so cool."

"That's not a common pet, and this isn't going to be your pet," Chelsea said.

"I practically live here," Terra said. "So it should be my pet, too."

"It can be your pet too, Terra, and I just thought of the perfect pet," I said. "We should get a puppy."

"That's a brilliant idea," my mom said. "What kind of dog were you thinking of?"

"Any kind of dog would be fine with me," I said. I took a minute to consult with everyone about the plan, and they all agreed.

On that same afternoon, we all went to a nearby pet shelter to look for a dog. The only problem was that the pet shelter wasn't exactly nearby. It was almost an hour drive. My mom didn't want to make the trip again, so se said that we had to pick out a pet on the same day.

When we were at the pet shelter, all the dogs were very happy to see people. It seemed that every breed of dog was there.

"Okay guys," my mom said. "If you want to pick out a dog together, you all have to work together as a team. Everyone must agree with the dog chosen."

Picking out a dog wasn't that hard. We only had to see one dog. It was a teacup poodle. It was a little big for a poodle, but that was what we liked about her.

"She's so cute," I said.

"How do you know it's a girl?" Kelly asked.

"I checked under her leg," I said. "Hey guys, get over here."

Terra examined the dog, and then said, "I don't know. I was thinking about getting a dog that's sportier. What's so sporty about a poodle?"

"Maybe we can teach her some tricks, so she'll seem sporty," I said, but I wasn't even sure if you could teach any tricks to a poodle.

My mom got the adoption papers since she noticed that everyone enjoyed the dog. "Okay kids, we need to pick a name for the dog." Then she said in a lower voice to the person at the counter, "This is going to take a while."

"How about naming it Friend?" Kelly asked.

"This dog isn't going to be your best friend," I said.

Chelsea started to look like she was really thinking, but then she said, "I've got nothing."

"We need a name that shows it's a girl, and that's it's sporty, and maybe how it looks," Woody said.

"I've got it," I said. "I know the perfect name."

"Stop thinking about it and tell us," Chelsea said.

"We should name the dog Miss Big Sport," I said.

Everyone thought about the name and looked at the dog. The dog just sat there staring back at us.

"Are we agreeing that the name is Miss Big Sport?" my mom asked us.

"Yeah," we all said almost at the same time.

While we were all at the pet shelter, my mom bought dog food and a pet taxi. We even bought her a tag, where all three of our addresses were on. Getting Miss Big Sport into the pet taxi wasn't easy. Chelsea tried to pick her up and shove her in, but she bit her. Terra also tried, but didn't succeed. Woody and Kelly were too scared to try. I knew a better way.

"Hey Miss Big Sport," I said. "Get in the pet taxi." Surprisingly, Miss Big Sport did get in the pet taxi.

"Have you met this dog before?" my mom asked.

"No," I said. "I haven't even been in this pet shelter before." But then I realized that I did meet that dog.

"It's the skate park dog!" Woody, Terra and I all said that at the same time.

"What are you guys talking about?" my mom asked.

"This dog caused me to fall," I said. "I know I said that I never wanted to see the dog again, but it helped me to walk again. This dog is a life saver. It probably got caught by pet control."

"I have an idea!" Kelly said as she ran in the pet shelter. When she noticed that we already got the dog in the pet taxi, she said, "Never mind."

"Okay," my mom said. "Let's go home with our new dog."

When we got home, I asked, "Is Miss Big Sport an indoor or an outdoor dog?"

"According to the adoption papers, she's both," my mom said, "and she's a pedigree, so she can enter in a dog show."

"She's only a puppy," I said, "and it's not like there are any dog shows coming soon. We'll just treat her like a member of the family."

CHAPTER 19:

The Dog Show

We all went to the living room where the TV was on. "I guess I forgot to turn off the TV before we left," my mom said. I was about to turn off the TV, but a commercial came on that caught everyone's attention.

On TV, there was a man holding a small dog. He said, "Do you have a dog? Does it know any tricks? If it does, enter it in the annual county dog show. This year's prize money is $5,000. Go to our website for more information. While you're there, sign up your dog today!"

In a minute, Chelsea was able to get on the website. We all agreed to let Miss Big Sport be in the dog show, so Chelsea signed her up. None of us cared about the prize money since we were rich.

"She's in the dog show," Chelsea said. "There's only one problem. The dog show's on the other side of L.A."

"That's okay," my mom said. "We're rich now. We can afford anything."

"I just thought of another problem," I said. "She doesn't know any tricks."

"That's why we got her," Terra said. "The only reason I agreed to care for her. My part was to train her to do some tricks, which is what I can do on the weekends"

"What about the skate park?" I asked.

"If you learn fast, I'll cut back on your training hours," Terra said.

"I want to help too, Kelly said.

"Sure," I said. "Woody, you can help if you want."

"What if she doesn't like me?" Woody asked.

"Then I guess you won't help," I said.

"Let's get back to the point," Chelsea said. "What tricks are we going to teach her?"

After Chelsea said that, I knew what tricks to teach Miss Big Sport. "Well, we can teach her how to go through an obstacle course for dogs. I know we don't have an actual obstacle course, but the skate park is perfect."

The week went by and it was finally Saturday. When I went to the skate park with Terra, we took Miss Big Sport with us. We had to be there before the skate perk opened so no one would interrupt our training. I was right when I said that the skate park was an obstacle course. Terra and I just had to put out a few things from the nearby dumpster. This obstacle course had a few tunnels to go through, a ramp to walk over, and those pole things that dogs zigzag through.

At first, Miss Big Sport had a hard time to go through the course, so it was a good thing that Terra put Miss Big Sport on a skateboard and pushed her through the first tunnel. She easily went through the rest of the course. The only problem was that she crashed into the poles. It's possible that Terra put rails near the poles so Miss Big Sport would automatically go through the poles.

"That seems like cheating," I said.

"No," Terra said. "She'll just use them for practice. After a few more tries with the rails, we'll take them away and she'll skate through them perfectly."

When our dog's training was over, my mom drove to the skate park to take her home. "How was the training?" she asked. I told her everything that we did except for the rigged poles.

After my mom left, it was time to open the gates to the sate park. People flooded the park as my skate park queen training began. I had a lot to learn, considering that I missed three weekends in a row. The training was easier than I thought. I just had to learn skateboard tricks that only queens and kings had learned. I didn't realize how many tricks I had to learn. Some of the tricks were familiar because I had seen Terra do them a few times. At that time, Miss Big Sport's training was easier.

The weekend after that was pretty much the same. The only difference was that we did more work, since the dog show was on the next day. Terra and I did as much as we could and we also had to plan how we would get to the dog show. It took us a few minutes to come to the conclusion that we would take the bus.

The stadium for the dog show was so huge. I think it was huge to fit all the people and contestants. Then, it came to my attention that there was a lot of competition. Since the stadium was huge, my mom made sure we were all together at all times. She would have be heart broken if she lost Kelly, and I would have been heart broken if I lost Miss Big Sport.

We all knew that it was Chelsea's responsibility to keep an eye on Miss Big Sport. She did just that on the bus and at the check-in line at the stadium. Everything was going fine.

After we checked in, I asked Terra, "Do you think Miss Big Sport is ready?"

"Of course she's ready," Terra replied. "I even have everything she needs." Then Terra whispered in my ear, "I even have the rails for the poles."

After she said that, I fell into a shock. I couldn't believe that Terra would resort to cheating. I had always thought of Terra as a very innocent person. I wanted to sneak the rails out of her bag and hide them in a place where no one would find them. I wanted to speak up, but nothing came out when I opened my mouth. I did my best not to say anything to anyone.

My shock ended when my mom said, "We have half an hour until we take our seats in the stadium. What does everyone want to do?"

"I think Miss Big Sport should practice her special trick," I said.

"That's a good idea," Woody said. "What's the trick anyway? I've never seen it."

"You'll see," Terra said with an almost evil smile.

While Miss Big Sport was practicing, I said, "Maybe she can do it without the rails. I don't want her to win by cheating."

Terra quickly said, "No it isn't. She can do it with the rails. Don't say that, okay?"

I was glad that my mom wasn't there to hear Terra say that. I just wished that I had never heard that.

Half an hour later, my mom came back with Kelly, Chelsea, and Woody. "I'll put Miss Big Sport back in the pet taxi so she can rest for a while. I know how to wake her up when it's her turn." We all agreed with Chelsea's plan. As Chelsea put Miss Big Sport in her pet taxi, my mom petted her on her head and on her back.

When we got in the stadium, I said to Chelsea, "I'll take Miss Big Sport now. You can all go find your reserved seats." Then I turned to Terra and said, "I'll take her bag."

"Are you sure you won't need my help?" Terra asked.

"It's okay. I can handle everything."

"Okay, well, she's number twenty. Make sure she's wearing her number."

I was able to handle everything, including the number. Since Terra wasn't next to me backstage, I was able to prevent using the rails.

Miss Big Sport and I were number twenty, and considering how long the other dogs' talents were, Miss Big Sport had time to practice with the poles without the rails.

All the contestants were lined up numerically, so I was between numbers nineteen and twenty-one. Number twenty-one had the same pet taxi as mine. I made a huge mistake to trade dogs with number twenty-one. We didn't actually trade our dogs though. We just traded to look at the other person's dog. His dog was all feisty and mean, whereas Miss Big Sport was calm and nice. You can probably guess what happened, but I'll tell you. We both grabbed the wrong pet taxi.

I didn't notice this until I opened the pet taxi and the feisty little dog attacked me. The attack reminded me of the fights I'd had with Gretchen, except the dog was smaller than me.

I heard the announcer say, "Now for Shannon Bauber and Miss Big Sport." I heard the applause and I wanted to get up, but the dog was still on me growling. I thought that if I got up, the dog would destroy me. After a few seconds, the announcer said my name again. The feisty dog ran out a slightly opened door and its owner ran out after it. Miss Big Sport ran out of the pet taxi and started barking at the dog as it was running outside. After the third time of saying my name, the announcer sent security backstage, where they found Miss Big Sport barking and I was still lying on the ground. The security guard thought that Miss Big Sport had attacked me, so he got out a tranquilizer. He almost got Miss Big Sport, but she quickly ran outside. No one knew where she had run off to.

CHAPTER 20:

Where's my Dog?

After about a minute, everyone ran backstage to help me up. When I did, everyone was surrounding me, and making sure that I wasn't hurt. I was hurt, but I was only hurt with a few scratches and bruises. Chelsea, Terra, Woody, and I went out looking for Miss Big Sport. Kelly stayed behind with my mom because she thought that Kelly was too young to be out by herself. They both stayed at the stadium while they explained to the guard that Miss Big Sport was innocent and it was the other dog's fault.

We reminded ourselves that we were in LA, so Miss Big Sport could have run off anywhere. We checked all of the nearby streets. We even went inside some of the nearby stores to see if she ran inside a building. I started to lose hope, and I thought that she was lost forever, but after a while, Woody said, "During that half hour before we were in the stadium, your mom got a tracker for Miss Big Sport in case she got lost. That's why she was petting her so much before the dog show. She was making sure that the tracker was secure on her."

"That means if we get the tracker, we can find out where Miss Big Sport ran off to," I said. I couldn't wait to see her again, and I wanted to have a happy reunion with her. I stood there picturing the moment that I lay eyes on her and she jumps into my arms and licks my face, but that was just my fantasy. I honestly didn't know how soon it would be until that picture came true.

"I'll get the tracker from Mom," Chelsea said. "Everyone stay here. I'll be back really soon." As soon as she finished talking, she started to run toward the stadium, and we watched her run until she was out of our sight.

Chelsea must have been running fast because within a few minutes, she was back with the tracker in her hands. Even though we were only waiting for a few minutes, it felt longer than that. Time felt very crucial, and we knew that the tracker was going to help us. This tracker was very hi-tech, but it was very easy to use. All you had to do was press the button that said "find." Then, it gives you the country, state, city, and address. Next, it gives you very clear turn-by-turn directions from where you're standing if you press the button that says "directions." It was easy enough to use that Kelly would had understood it.

It was a good thing that Miss Big Sport was still in the area. She was definitely in walking distance. We were all a little concerned though. We noticed that she wasn't moving that much and mostly stayed where she was. I knew that we were going to find her okay, but I sometimes thought that she was dead, which would have explained why she wasn't moving. I tried to think about the positives about her by thinking that she was asleep or maybe that her instincts had let her known that we were looking for her.

We spent a little less than half an hour looking for Miss Big Sport. When the tracker said that we found her, we thought that it was malfunctioning. "What's wrong with this thing?" I asked with anger. I didn't understand why it was saying that we found her. She wasn't anywhere in front of us. That was the problem. I looked around at our surroundings. Then, I realized something very important. She wasn't in front of us because she was next to us in the middle of the street!

The happy reunion picture came back to me. All I wanted to do then was run out to Miss Big Sport and pull her off the street. I didn't see why not. We were in an empty neighborhood, so there were practically no cars around, and there were no passing cars at the time. So, I ran out to the street. Everyone tried to stop me, but I was too fast. When I ran out to her, she wasn't running to me. I didn't know why until I noticed that she stuck in a small hole. I pulled her as much as I could, and I got her out of the hole. I sat there for a few seconds while I brushed off the dirt from her. I took my time to grab her in my arms and I stood up.

Sadly, I was a little too late. A car was driving by and the driver didn't see me. I only had enough time to throw Miss Big Sport safely to the sidewalk, and she landed right next to Woody. You probably know what happened next. I tried to run, but I tripped over my own shoelaces and I fell. I did my best to get up as fast as I could, but I wasn't fast even. I got hit by the car. The driver stopped the car immediately after he felt the hit.

Woody was the first one to run to me, and everyone was staring down at me. I knew that he was running as fast as he could, but it looked as though he was running slowly. I knew I wasn't seeing how I was supposed to. Everything that I looked at seemed to move slower than it really was. He finally came to me. He picked me up and carried me to the sidewalk with a few tears in his eyes. He dropped to his knees as I saw everything spinning. My mom called 911. I was shortly in the hospital, where I fell asleep. I knew that I should have died when that car hit me, but it didn't. I thought that I was never going to see life again, but since it didn't, I had a feeling that I was going to die very soon.

CHAPTER 21:

Happy Anniversary

I woke up on a different day in the hospital. The room was empty. I was used to waking up surrounded by people, so it was surprising to me when no one was there. I thought I was paralyzed again, and I was right. This time, I was paralyzed from the waist down. From my last experience, I considered myself lucky.

I had expected to wake up in my dad's old room, and I did. Everything was the same like. Nothing was moved since the day that I came by to pick up my boxes. I was surprised that no one had moved anything.

Woody ran in the room. He ran to me and gave me a very tight hug, and I was able to hug him back. He said, "I'm glad that you're alive."

"So am I," I said with a smile.

"Do you know what day it is?" He let go of me so I could look over at the calendar. Then, he took a small box out of his pocket as he said, "Happy anniversary."

I couldn't believe it. I was in my longest coma that lasted until Valentine's Day, which was our one-year anniversary since we started dating. While some couples could only be together for a month, we had been together for a year. I knew that there was a reason for why I woke up on the right day. I opened the box that Woody gave me. It was gold, so I knew right away that it was jewelry. I picked up the jewelry to find out that it was a golden necklace with a heart on it.

"Open the heart," he said.

When I opened the heart, it had a picture of my dad. It was the same picture that was on the table next to me. There was a note next to the picture on the other side of the heart. It was in my dad's original hand writing and it said, "Paralyzed or not, we can get through anything."

"That's what your dad's last words were," Woody said. "He said that before his vocal cords died out permanently. Remember, he was paralyzed below the neck just like you."

Then, Woody did something that I had rarely ever seen him do. He started to cry. I wasn't sure until I asked him, "Are you crying?"

He didn't need to answer. All I did was hug him. I had never seen Woody get so emotional, but I knew that death was something hard for him to think about, which was why he was so concerned about me.

I continued to hug him until his tears lightened up. When he stopped crying and his face was dried, Terra and Chelsea walked in the room. Terra said, "I told your mom about the rigged poles. I now know what I did was wrong. I'm glad that Miss Big Sport didn't perform after all. I heard that some other guy did the exactly the same thing, and he got disqualified. That could have happened to us. Either way, we had no chance of winning."

"You know you're going to need a new queen of the skate park," I said.

"Is it possible that we can drop you from a high building and see if a miracle happens?"

"It's too risky, and it's different this time. I'm paralyzed from the waist down instead of from the neck. Falling might make it worse."

"Okay, so do you have any ideas on who will be princess?"

"Don't you mean prince?" I pointed to Woody.

Terra turned to Woody and shook his hand. "Congratulations Woody, you're going to be the new prince of the skate park."

"Are you serious?" Woody asked.

"Heck yeah," Terra said. "Don't worry, I'll teach you everything you need to know. Even though you don't know much about skateboarding, I know that you're a fast learner, and you've seen Shannon skate for years. I know you're scared about the risks, but you're older now. If you know what you're doing, you won't get hurt. You'll be a perfect prince. Your training starts on Saturday afternoon."

Woody was so excited that he couldn't talk. When he did talk, it was completely off subject. He asked, "Shannon, what are we going to do for our anniversary? You can choose what we do and where we go."

"I know where we can go."

Woody liked the idea I gave him, so we went with it as soon as the ivy was taken out of my arm and the bandages were taken off my head. We went to the skate park so everyone knew what happened. Of course, Terra came along with us and we all skated.

When we got to the skate park, Terra made the announcement saying that Woody was the new prince of the skate park. Just to show how good he was, she forced him on the half pipe and pushed him off so everyone knew what he was capable of doing. She also explained how he would improve. He was wearing padding, so he wasn't hurt.

After Woody did his performance, the geek came up to me. It was the same geek who exposed my paralysis a month ago. Anyway, the geek told me of different ways that I could skateboard on my hands, and my legs wouldn't be a factor. At first, he used the hard words that that only nerds could understand. Then, he put it into smaller words that a normal person could understand. He even showed me a video of hand skating on his laptop. Yes, that time he had a laptop.

Twenty minutes later, Terra said, "I know she's a little paralyzed, but she'll show you what she can do using her hands. Yeah, it's possible."

When I was skateboarding, everything felt better. I had no worries. I didn't even worry about falling. That was a sure sign that I belonged in the skate park. That was the best first anniversary ever, and I knew that I would never forget it. After all that I went through, I was glad that something stayed the same, and I was glad that it was skateboarding. Life felt perfect.

EPILOGUE:

Nine Years Later

It's been nine years since I thought life was perfect, and I still believe that life almost feels perfect. It has also been nine years since those events happened, and I love to look back at my childhood. Now, I am a twenty-two year old adult and I look like a young Heather Locklear, except I skateboard instead act. After I graduated from college, I became a famous skateboarder, and that career has been working out for me. I also know other famous skateboarders, like Woody and Terra. Terra was right. If you're king or queen of the Los Angeles skate park, you become famous. I know that Woody was picked to be king, but Terra made an exception. Woody and I reigned together as king and queen until we turned eighteen. Of course, we chose a good teen to take our place and we started a new rule that a king and queen can rule together. Anyway, during our last year, scouts came by to see our skating. They liked what they saw, we both signed a contract, and we became famous.

Another very special thing happened right after I graduated. On the same day that we got our diplomas, Woody asked me to marry him. Of course, I said yes. Our wedding was very different. It was a big wedding, but not a big white wedding. Just about all of our guests were skateboarders. The other guests were my mom, Chelsea and her husband, and Kelly and her boyfriend. I even invited the geek from the skate park and his equally geeky girlfriend. The best part about getting married was the honeymoon, which was at the X-games, where I appear every year.

It's still a surprise to me that I stayed with Woody for all those years, when it was almost impossible for us to continue dating. After we graduated from junior high, my mom tried to force me into an all-girl private school when she noticed that I barely had the grades to pass. She thought that I would get better grades if I wasn't distracted by boys. At the same time, Woody almost had to move out of the state. We didn't want that to happen. So, we had got people to sign petitions to keep Woody in the state and to keep me in public school.

I have decided to stay paralyzed from the waist down for my entire life. Even when I was offered an operation so I could walk again, I just turned it down. I know I had the money. My mom and my sisters also had the money. If I had the surgery, I wouldn't be able to skate board on my hands anymore. That's what made me famous.

I kept Miss Big Sport for all those years as well. She never performed her trick again. She never entered in a dog show. Actually, I never let her. She didn't do anything related to a talent or trick. She was still a good dog though.

It's a year after I got married, and we have just bought the perfect house to spend the rest of our lives in, and it's perfect for the children we are going to adopt. Throughout those years, I still have my necklace from my first anniversary. I still had those words in my head forever. "Paralyzed or not, we can get through anything."